TRAILBLAZERS
Poems of Exploration

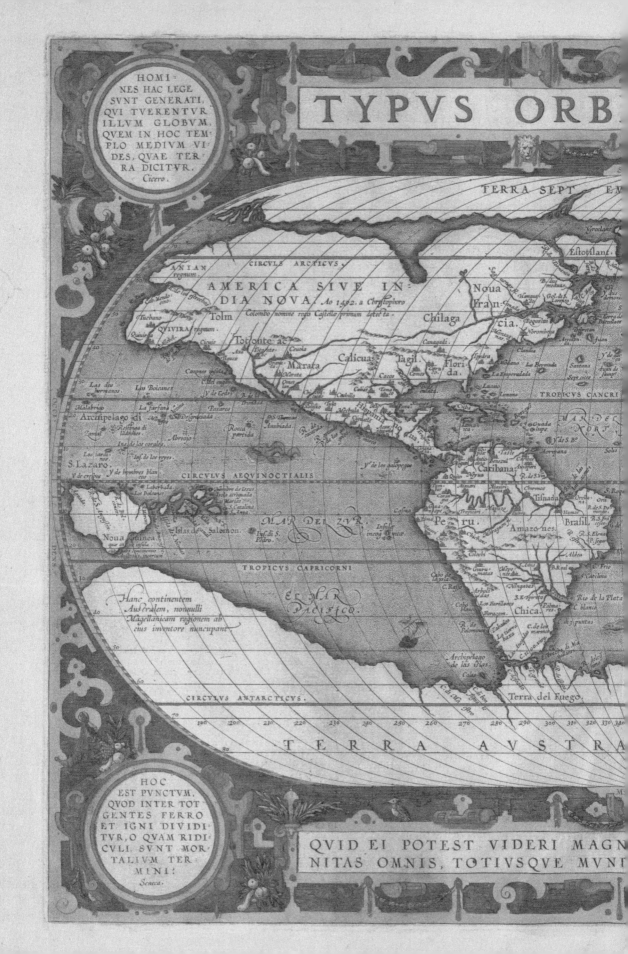

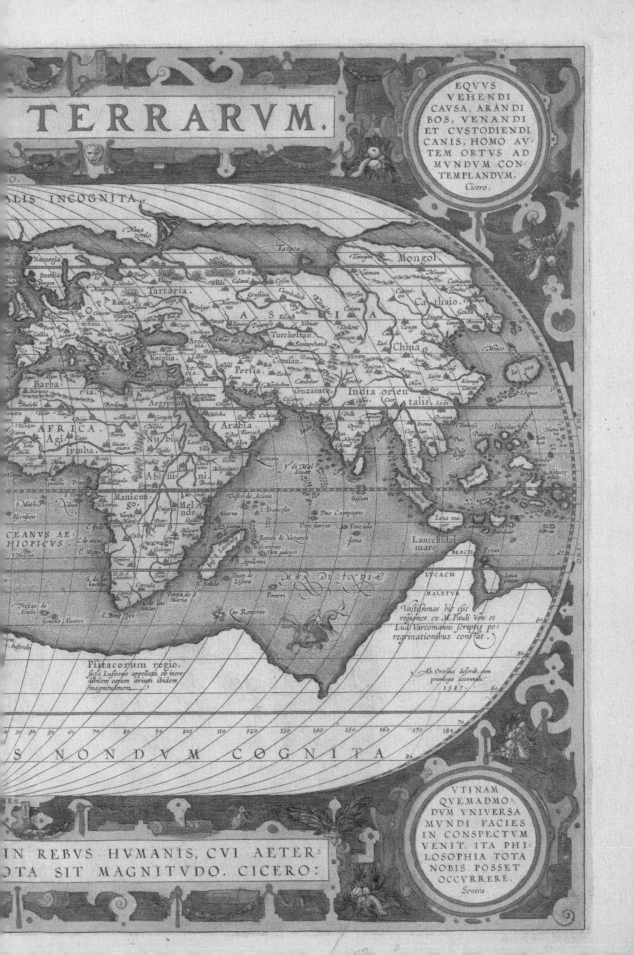

TRAILBLAZERS
Poems of Exploration

By Bobbi Katz

Illustrations by Carin Berger

Greenwillow Books
An Imprint of HarperCollins Publishers

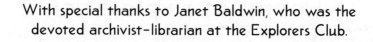

With special thanks to Janet Baldwin, who was the devoted archivist-librarian at the Explorers Club.

Trailblazers: Poems of Exploration
Text copyright © 1993, 2001, 2007 by Bobbi Katz.
Illustrations copyright © 2007 by Carin Berger.

The text of this book is set in Pacific Clipper and Stemple Garamond.
Book design by Victoria Jamieson

Typus orbis terrarum. [1595]. Engravings—hand-colored. Abraham Ortelius. I.N. Phelps Stokes Collection, Miriam and Ira D. Wallach Division of Art, Prints and Photographs, The New York Public Library, Astor, Lenox and Tilden Foundations.

Library of Congress Cataloging-in-Publication Data
Katz, Bobbi.
Trailblazers: poems of exploration / by Bobbi Katz.
p. cm.
"Greenwillow Books."
Includes bibliographical references.
ISBN-13: 978-0-688-16533-8 (trade bdg.) ISBN-10: 0-688-16533-8 (trade bdg.)
ISBN-13: 978-0-688-16534-5 (lib. bdg.) ISBN-10: 0-688-16534-6 (lib. bdg.)
1. Explorers—Juvenile poetry. 2. Historical poetry, American. 3. Children's poetry, American.
4. Explorers—Biography—Juvenile literature. I. Title.
PS3561.A7518T73 2007 811'. 54—dc22 2006016696

First Edition 10 9 8 7 6 5 4 3 2 1

 Greenwillow Books

For Her Deepness,
Sylvia A. Earle, PhD

Why Explore?

Think of oceans.
Think of rivers.
      Think of spices.
         Think of space.
Think of greed
    for gold and glory
        or the lure of a new place.
Think of longing for adventure.
Think of yearning to learn more.
Think what beckons,
        beckons,
           beckons!
Think what's saying,
"Go explore!"

TABLE OF CONTENTS

Adam and Eve

The Lord God took the man and placed him in the garden of Eden, to till it and tend it. And the Lord God commanded the man, saying, "Of every tree of the garden you are free to eat; but as for the tree of knowledge of good and evil, you must not eat of it."

Genesis 2:15–17

The First Explorers
Adam and Eve: East of Eden, a long time ago

Adam:
We are banned from the Garden
With no hope of a pardon.
So, dear Eve, which way to go?

Yes, my dear, "out there" is here.
We've never been here before.

No guide. We are quite alone.

That apple!

An appetite for knowledge?
Can I be hearing right?

Eve:
We are banned from the garden
With no hope of a pardon.

How am I supposed to know?
Now we're "out there."

We've never been here before.

Our taste of knowledge left
so much unknown.
That apple!
How I'd like to take another bite.
I'm left with such an appetite.

Eve, He made us leave,
for just one bite.

Exactly.
And if we had taken two
what more could He do?
If we had taken three
it seems to me
we'd know much more.
And four . . .

It was so nice in Paradise.
You got us in this mess, dear Eve.
Which way to go?

Let's see where this river flows.
Let's follow this river.
Let's see where it goes.
Who knows where it will end?
Another
Eden
  might be
      just
    around
      the
        bend.

Preface

As you read these words, hundreds of miles above Earth, the Hubble Telescope, and other newer telescopes, are roving eyes of the universe, peering into what seem to be ever-expanding heavens. It is discovering nurseries of baby stars—whole new galaxies—as far as nine billion light years away! I certainly can't get my mind around a billion jelly beans, let alone a billion light years, but I do know it is far, very, *very* far, a distance that dwarfs measurements here on Earth. Yet it was human beings—individuals wired just like the men and women who created the Hubble Telescope—who over the past centuries explored our little green planet and not so long ago made the first sorties into outer space. Their bodies and brains were—and are—basically like yours and mine.

Through poems based on diaries, journals, historical accounts, biographies, ancient sagas, and contemporary magazine and newspaper articles, I've tried to bring some of these explorers and travelers into your lives. Whenever possible I've woven some of their very own words into my poems. Hopefully, I've helped reveal people whom you will admire, detest, love, fear, empathize with, envy, or want to know better. Real people—not paper dolls.

Queen Hatshepsut

History's first great woman ruler, although not Egypt's first woman head of state, was the widow of Pharaoh Thutmose II. She ruled for over twenty years and built a magnificent temple near Thebes.

Orders
Queen Hatshepsut: Deir al–Bahri, Egypt, 1493 BC

Right here, my master builder,
    you shall erect a colonnade
to honor my brave sailors
    for the voyage they have made.
For did they not at my command
    sail off to Punt, that distant land?
And did they not return with trees
    whose incense Egypt's gods will please?
And being pleased by scent of myrrh,
    will not the gods my death defer?
Show these men with trees in hand
    so those to come will understand
men faced the terrors of the sea,
    to please the gods . . .
    and so please me.

Hanno of Carthage

Imagine being a teenager on an expedition to settle thousands of Carthaginians along the coast of Africa and then to continue south, where even Hanno had not yet sailed.

My Story
Pele of Carthage: 530 BC

My parents and my grandparents,
  my brothers, sisters, cousins,
    my uncle who can play the flute,
      our neighbors by the dozens,
        we all sailed off for Africa
          with Hanno's mighty fleet
            past the Pillars of Herakles,
            not knowing what we might meet.
For we were sent to build new towns,
where Carthage then could trade.
Strong boys like me were thrilled to go.
The old and frail were afraid:
    "What if our seeds from home won't grow
    where they've *never* been planted before?"
"What if native Africans show
it's not trade they want. It's war!"
    "What if our gods cannot hear us,
    when we pray from a place far away?"

"What if . . . ?"

"What if . . . ?"

"What if . . . ?"

"What if . . . ?"

That's *all* those elders could say.

In two days, we stopped at a harbor,
where four ships and their passengers stayed.
Hanno named the place Altar of Incense.
And I'm *sure* the gods heard when we prayed!
When we sailed local people came with us.
We learned their words,

as they learned ours:

by pointing

and then by repeating:

SEA . . . BIG . . .

SKY . . . BLUE . . .

MOON . . . STARS . . .

On down the coast we traveled,
leaving settlers at points Hanno chose.
In all he would plant seven cities.
And that would be fine, I suppose.
But oh, how I wished to continue
exploring the African shore.
The sight of elephants feeding
only made me want to see more.

Hanno said that he could use me,
if I would work like a man.
"Father," I begged, "please let me stay!"
At last he agreed that I can!

I'll leave my family at Arambys.
        May their home be my home some day.
        But for now
                I'll sail down the African coast.
                What will I see
                        on the way?

Alexander the Great

When Alexander swept through Persia, Egypt, and Asia Minor, most of his soldiers' families traveled along with the army. Penelope speaks from Afghanistan, where Alexander's conquests finally stopped.

Returning Home

Penelope, daughter of Crateros: the Makran Desert, 325 BC

Their story changes with each retelling of it.
I was three years old when my family left our home.
I do not know the grape-heavy vineyards,
nor have I favorites among the sure-footed goats.
My parents' memories of springtime rites aren't mine.
Home, safe place of peace and quiet.
Just imagine!
Clash of sword and dagger,
    screaming wounded,
       burning cities:
These are the things I know.
    These are my memories.
Alexander, who would be god of all nations,
leads us home across this godforsaken desert.
No food.
    No water.
       Air so hot we must march by night.

Mouth dry.
        Stomach empty.
Yet pictures fill my mind.
I hope to know the vineyards,
        the sure-footed goats.
That safe place of peace and quiet, home.
Just imagine!

Egeria

A remarkable nun, who was clearly a person of importance, kept a diary in the form of letters of her three-year pilgrimage to Egypt, Byzantium, and most important, the Holy Land.

A Letter to Galicia
Egeria: Palestine, circa 390

My dear sisters in Christ our God,
May you follow the Exodus with me
from the heights of Mount Sinai
where Moses once stood
to Mount Nebo where he died.
But should you wish to know more
About the pillar of salt,
which Lot's wife became,
I cannot offer any details.
Our guide shows us the place
where Lot's wife,
    turning back
        toward the flaming city
        where she once lived
        was punished by the Lord.
"Until recently," he points out,
"the pillar stood here."

Yet ladies, "For many a year,"
or so the Bishop of Segor tells me,
"waters have covered the pillar."
Sisters, it may be salting the Dead Sea!
An amazing thought, is it not?

Vikings

Long before Erik the Red settled Greenland and his son Leif Eriksson may have wintered in North America, their ancestors struck England, Ireland, Wales, and later Europe with lightning speed. What was it like to be a Viking?

Summer Sport
Helge Ingveld: near the Irish coast, 790

Pillage, plunder,
   rampage, rob.
     I'm a Viking!
       That's my job.
         Vikings become
           better workers
             when they're roused
          to be berserkers.
       Our nimble boats
   with prows that soar
can speed us
   to some distant shore,
       where we serve Odin, god of War.
         Booty—more than we can carry—
           waits in some hapless monastery.
       How can it be
     the monks don't learn
     that every summer we return?

As surely as their gardens flower,
　　Vikings strike with stunning power.
As surely as their trees bear fruit,
　　Vikings harvest summer loot.
　　　　And like
　　　　　a summer storm,
　　　　　our thunder
　　　　　terrifies . . .
　　　　　before
　　　　　we
　　　　　plunder.

Rabbi Benjamin Ben Jonah of Tudela

Rabbi Benjamin left his home in northern Spain and traveled as far as China and Tibet, commenting on Jewish life in each place he visited.

A Tale of Two Cities
Rabbi Benjamin of Tudela: 1157

Constantinople:
The circumference of the city is eighteen miles:
half of it upon the sea,
                        half upon the land.
Here is the church of Santa Sophia,
with pillars of gold and silver
and more gold and silver lamps
than any man can count.
It is the seat of the Pope of the Greeks.
        Tribute flows to Constantinople
from every part of the Empire of Greece
        and from merchants who come by land or sea
                from Babylon, Persia, and Egypt,
                from the land of Canaan and the empire of Russia,
                        from Hungaria and Khazaria,
                                Lombardy and Sepharad. . . .
Small wonder the Greeks go about like princes
in garments of silk with gold embroidery!
King Emanuel, the Emperor, has built a great palace
wherein is set a throne of gold and precious stones.

The sparkle of his crown is said to be so bright
        that even in the dark of night
     there is no need for further light.

No Israelites may live in Constantinople.
They are shut off by an inlet of the sea
        in a district called Pera.
They cannot come or go except by boat.
Nor is a Jew allowed to ride a horse,
        except (of course)
Solomon Hamitari, physician to the king.
The Jews, good and bad alike,
are subjected to beatings for no reason.
Yet they remain charitable
and make the best of their oppression.

Baghdad:
The circumference of the city is twenty miles,
extending to both shores of the river Tigris.
Here is the royal residence of the Caliph,
Emir al Muminin al Abbasi of the family of Mohammed,
whom all the kings of Islam must obey
and all of Islam's imams as well,
as Christian priests obey the Pope.
The Caliph is truthful and trustworthy,
speaking peace to all men.
His palace is within a great walled park.
Waters of the Tigris fill its lake.

When the Caliph wishes to feast,
his servants have but to catch
all manner of birds and game and fish.
The Caliph issues forth but once a year,
        wearing gold and silver royal robes
and a turban, adorned with priceless gems.
He rides a mule.
Over his turban is a modest black shawl,
        a reminder that death and darkness come to all.
The princes of Islam from Persia to Tibet
        accompany him on horses,
            along roads adorned
                with silk and purple,
                    filled with the singing of joyful people.
            Entering the great mosque
                near the Basrah Gate
                    the Caliph mounts the pulpit.
                        Blessing everyone,
                        he expounds on the laws of Islam,
                then sacrifices a camel, which is distributed.

Under the Great Caliph, a most benevolent man,
Israelites dwell in security, prosperity, and honor.

Genghis Khan

Jebe and Subedi were commanders of Genghis Khan's army of exploration and . . . conquest.

The Plan of the Mongol Commanders
Russia: May 1223

Jebe:
We're outnumbered four to one.

> *Subedi:*
>
> *Shall we pretend we're on the run?*

A fine idea! We'll feign retreat.
They'll be sure that when we meet
our smaller force will taste defeat.

> *They'll grow careless as they chase,*
> *letting space between their troops erase*
> *the advantage they have in one place. . . .*

And that's when we will swerve around.
Then Russian blood will stain the ground.

> *Riding at a fearful pace,*
> *we'll celebrate the Mongol race!*
> *Each archer on his well-trained mare*
> *will blizzard arrows through the air,*

Our horses and our cavalry
will be our keys
to victory!

> *Our horses and our cavalry*
> *will be our keys*
> *to victory!*

Marco Polo

Mirella might have heard Marco Polo telling his fellow prisoner, the writer Rusticello, about his travels. Both men were from Venice, which was at war with the city-state of Genoa.

Can It Be So?
Mirella, the jailer's daughter: Genoa, 1298

I hear him tell such stories
that I hate to go away.
I could listen, listen, listen
to what he has to say all day.
He speaks of such strange creatures.
Could there be a crocodile,
which lives on land and water,
with dagger teeth that seem to smile?
He says that silk is made by worms.
It's *not* bark from a tree!
Did Marco Polo make that up?
He sounds sincere to me.
The Emperor, called Kublai Khan,
has forty-seven sons
and lots and lots of extra wives,
especially pretty ones.
Oh, how I would like to go
to China and Tibet.
Marco Polo has seen more
than any man I've met.

Ibn Battuta

The Sultan of Morocco ordered the poet Ibn Juzayy to record the Rihla, *or, story of Ibn Battuta. Supposedly, he had traveled 75,000 miles, three times more than Marco Polo.*

From *The Rihla of Ibn Battuta*
by Ibn Juzayy: Fez, 1354

When I was but a child,
seeds of twin desires
took root in my heart:
  to make the *hajj*, the pilgrimage to Mecca,
  to visit Medina, site of the Prophet's tomb.
As I grew, so grew they.
At age twenty-one,
I braced myself to quit my dear ones.
Forsaking home,
  as birds forsake their nests,
I left Tangier,
  alone
   on a donkey:
    without family
     without friends.
But I found generosity.
Scholars shared their thoughts with me.
  Some offered hospitality
Time was never an object.

I spent one day drinking tea with a mystic,
Sheikh Abu Abdullah al Murshidi.
That night as I slept on the roof above his cell,
I dreamt a dream. I remember it well:
      On the wing of a huge bird I flew toward Mecca,
          next toward the Yemen,
              then
after flying and flying toward the east—
      such a long, long flight—
the huge bird at last chose to alight
      in some dark greenish country.
          It left me there.
Amazingly, the Sheikh knew of my dream!
It was a map of my future, showing God's intent:
      first the *hajj,* then the far-most reaches of the Orient!
Provisioning me with cakes and silver coins,
      the mystic sent me on my way.
          I soon joined a caravan
              of traders and pilgrims
                 on horseback
                 on camels
                    on donkeys like me
                    and many on foot.
We were a constantly growing company:
first like a large household,
      then a village, and finally . . . a city,
moving, moving,
      mile after mile,

over mountains,
      through forests,
         across deserts
            toward Algiers,
         toward Tunis,
      toward Alexandria,
   toward Cairo,
toward Damascus,
   toward Medina,
      City of the Apostle of God
         and . . . at last . . .
            with hearts full of gladness
            arriving
         at the goal of our hopes, Mecca!

Zheng He

The third emperor of the Ming Dynasty wanted China to extend its influence and to learn about the world and sent Zheng He on ambitious expeditions. However, the next Ming emperor was influenced by courtiers who felt Chinese values were best served by isolation.

At the Emperor's Court
Two Confucian scholars: China, 1432

Zheng He has too much power.
Let us stop him, please.
There is no need for China
to sail to distant seas,
to have a huge armada
with such splendid ships as these.
Ships in such great numbers.
Let us stop him, please!

For centuries our sailors sailed
to India and then
they traveled on to Africa
and sailed back home again.
But Zheng He has built treasure ships.
Nine masts reach for the sky
with red silk sails to catch the wind.
Why, I ask, but why?

There's nothing
in the outside world
that China needs to know.
Why spend and spend
on ships to sail
where there's no need to go?

There's nothing
in the outside world
that China needs to know.
Why spend and spend
on ships to sail
where there's no need to go?

Henry the Navigator

It was not unusual for royalty to be given personal servants close to their own ages from the time they left the care of a nursemaid. Perhaps Prince Henry had such a servant.

Remembering Prince Henry
An unidentified servant: Sagres, Cape St. Vincent, Portugal, 1460

I

Ruined

    were the roads of the Romans.

Lost

    were the maps of the Greeks.

Forgotten

    the skills of Phoenicians,

    who ventured to sea with large fleets.

Found

    were the maps drawn by Ptolemy

    with his books written centuries ago.

Snared

    was my young lord, Prince Henry,

    obsessed by a passion to know.

II

Sagres became Prince Henry's school,

    a magnet for navigators,

for builders of bigger and better boats,

for sea instrument creators.
"Sailors,
    map-makers,
        students of stars,
come tell us what you can tell!"
Henry queried the sages of Islam
    and wise Jewish scholars as well.
He bought every map
    that money could buy.
        He studied.
            He questioned.
                He learned.
The world did not end at Bojador!
His men sailed beyond . . .
    and returned!

III

I served him not quite fifty years,
    almost half a century.
He opened windows to the world
    for Portugal . . .
        and . . .
            for me.

Christopher Columbus

Toscanelli was an outstanding Italian astronomer, geographer, and generous correspondent. One of his pen pals was his countryman, Columbus.

A Letter to Cristobal Columbus
Paolo dal Pozzo Toscanelli: Florence, 1474

Greetings to you, Worthy Sir,
    I applaud your grand wish to go
    to find those lands,
    those wondrous lands,
    where precious spices grow.
    Martinez of Portugal,
    a favorite of the king,
    has set his heart, as you might know,
    upon that very thing.
    So I send you the same sea chart
    as I recently sent to him
    with a letter
    in which I suggest
    the way to reach the East that's best
    is to set your compass
        toward
          the West.
    May Good Fortune smile on you.
    May you accomplish what you wish to do.

Paolo dal Pozzo Toscanelli

Christopher Columbus

After Ferdinand of Aragon married Queen Isabella of Castile, they united their two kingdoms. Although by this time many savants thought the world was round, perhaps the king did not.

King Ferdinand's Remarks
Spain, 1490

"My lovely Queen, dear Isabella,
who is this crass Columbus fellow,
hanging out here at our palace,
drinking from the royal chalice?
Is that pompous paragon
some relative from Aragon?
A distant cousin from Castile
freeloading for a royal meal?
His accent is too strange to place.
His manners lack a courtly grace.
He argues with our scientists:
'The world is round!' So he insists.
'The world is round!' Imagine that—
when everybody knows it's flat!

My lovely Queen, dear Isabella,
let's rid Spain of this pesky fellow.
Equip the scamp to sail the sea.
Give him a ship or two or three.

Then when he reaches the world's edge
his ships will cower on the ledge.
Sea serpents dreadful to behold
will make Columbus far less bold,
and if he's lucky he'll return
humble, modest, taciturn.
'The world is round.' Imagine that,
when *everybody* knows it's flat!"

Vasco da Gama

In 1498 da Gama brought the Zamorin, the ruler of Calicut, a letter from King Manuel of Portugal. It offered friendship.

What Manner of Men Are These?
The Zamorin of Calicut, India, 1502

From the very first whiff, da Gama smelled of danger.
Tasting caution in my own words, I hoped he did not hear fear.
How the Muslim traders railed against the Christians!
If Muslims, Jews, and Hindus profit by peaceful trade,
      why not these Portuguese?

Tasting caution in my own words, I hoped da Gama did not hear fear.
I gave him a letter for his king, a friendly business offer.
If Muslims, Jews, and Hindus profit by peaceful trade,
      why not these Portuguese?
India's gems and spices for Portugal's scarlet cloth and silver.

I gave him a letter for his king, a friendly business offer.
Da Gama sailed home with samples of cloves, ginger, pepper.
Portugal's scarlet cloth and silver for India's gems and spices.
But now da Gama returns with warships to trade with fire
      and with blood.

Da Gama sailed home with samples of cloves, ginger, pepper.
How the Muslim traders railed against the Christians!
But now da Gama returns with warships to trade with fire
        and with blood.
From the very first whiff, da Gama smelled of danger.

Vasco Núñez de Balboa

A ruthless adventurer, Balboa used torture and a pack of vicious dogs to terrify the Indians into giving him gold. They told him of a great South Sea with fabulously rich land beyond it.

With Leóncico at My Golden Sea

Vasco Núñez de Balboa: Darien, Panama, September 25, 1513

I

There's never been a richer dog
        than my Leóncico.
He joins our raiding missions,
        no matter where we go.
When we divide the booty—
        like any soldier there—
my brave dog, Leóncico,
        gets an equal share.

II

I learned of boundless treasure
        beyond the great South Sea;
I learned his Majesty, the King,
        planned on replacing . . . me!
If I could reach the great South Sea
        and claim it for the King

31

I knew he'd be quite willing
        To give me anything.
Presto, vamos a la selva,
        where the howler monkey cries.
Soldiers, porters! *Presto! Presto!*
        There's no time to pack supplies.
Yes, men, hurry to the jungle!
        You'll get gold and you'll get rich,
            (if an arrow doesn't kill you,
                if you don't die in a ditch,
                    if a serpent doesn't bite you
                        or squeeze you in its deadly hold . . .)
Presto! Hurry to the jungle!
        Follow me and you'll get gold!

I led the way across the swamps
        with my Leóncico.
He showed his teeth and growled his growl
        if someone seemed too slow.

III

One in three survived the trek.
They wait for us below
the mountain range I'm climbing
with my dog, Leóncico.

We see the sparkling waters
of the distant great South Sea,
The sunset waves are liquid gold
for Leóncico and me.
I didn't want another man
to stand with me up there.
I didn't want Leóncico
to have a smaller share.

Hernando Cortés

When Montezuma, the Aztec king, heard about Cortés and his horses, he believed the god Quetzalcoatl was returning as legend had promised. Cortés knew about the legend and exploited it.

Voices Heard on the Way to Tenochtitlan
Mexico, 1519

Enrique Ayala, soldado
Cortés sent one ship back to Spain,
Then scuttled the four others.
We have no choice. No chance to leave.
We're *conquistadores*, brothers.

Alfonso Arenales, soldado
Treasure, treasure, treasure!
That's what we're here to get.
Eight long years in Cuba
with no sign of treasure, yet.

Pedro de Alvarado, soldado
Look, what's coming! What a sight!
Hernando Cortés got it right.
Gold and silver, flashing jewels.
They welcome us. They must be fools!

Montezuma's Emissary

Back from the kingdom of the Sun,
Quetzalcoatl, holy one!
Welcome, welcome from our king!
Precious garments now we bring,
Your temple is in readiness.
You whom we honor, whom we bless.
Welcome, welcome from our king.

Hernando Cortés

Here's what your god says you must do:
Bring me your gold, your silver, too.
Tell Montezuma if he's slow,
rivers of Aztec blood will flow.
So *presto*, hurry, tell your king,
"God's here

      and god wants . . .

           everything."

Ferdinand Magellan

The lively diary of this pious Italian nobleman details Magellan's expedition around the world.

- ▬ ▬ ▬ ▬ ▲ ▬ ▬ ▬ ▬ ▬

The Voyage of Magellan diary entries:
Antonio Pigafetta, August 1519–September 6, 1522

August 1519
Spanish flags were flying
> as the five ships sailed away
> > with two hundred thirty-seven men
> > on a brilliant August day.
We stopped
> at the Canaries,
> > Cape Verde,
> > > then Brazil.
The North Star disappeared from sight.
> > A cross took a place
> in the sky each night!
> A cross in the sky:
> a sign to see,
> > a call to Christianity!
> > It would be easy
> to convert these people.
And oh, what delicious fruits grow in Brazil.

February 1520

May the son of God, Jesus,
guide His servant, Magellan
to better do His work.
We entered the Río de Plata,
which Magellan said
      would lead us
         to the great ocean in the West.
              Now
         after three weeks
   we return
  to the river's mouth,
for it was finally clear
      Río de Plata had *no* intent
of letting us sail
      across this continent.
       Sailing south
        it grows cold,
    so very cold.
Sea geese appear.
Like gentleman
severely dressed in black and white,
they make a most amazing sight.
They stand in groups so numerous,
less like birds
      more . . . like us.
And sea wolves rove here
     stranger yet

than any wolves our hunters get.
With heads so smooth
                front legs like wings
        they dive and swim
like fishy things.
        Back legs pressed within a tail,
a sort of rudder
        or a sail.
On land the sea wolf is so slow.
Perhaps the cause is ice and snow.

March 1520–November 1521
Everything is upside down
in the southern world.
So it is when trees blossom in Europe,
icicles flower here.
Cold grips our ships
in its embrace.
We stay in a protected bay,
until October's end,
when winter's monotony is past.
It's spring at last
        and we sail free!

The Strait of Magellan
        Still going South—
one ship wrecked,
        another deserted—
when the land opens

and we sail
            into the proper
        waterway.
It broadens
            and
        narrows.
            It turns,
        twists
    and makes for a torturous trip.
Then the Lord rewards our navigator:
We sail into an ocean, calm and peaceful.
"The Pacific Ocean," says Magellan.
The tears he sheds are tears of joy.

March 1521
Joy was short-lived.
The next three months and twenty days
we had no chance to take on food.
Our biscuits swarmed with worms.
Our water was putrid.
The men ate the oxhide
that covered the main yard . . .
the sawdust from the boards.
Rats were sold for one ducado each.
Then there were no more
to be had
at any price.
Many men were sick or had died
by the time our fortunes changed,

and we reached the Ladrones,
the islands of the thieves.
We soon sailed off and claimed the Philippines.
The people were eager to be Christians.
As their friend, Magellan
went to fight with them
        against their foe.
I begged him to let me go
in his place,
But he said "No."
An arrow killed him.

With too few men to man three ships,
the *Concepción* was burned.

September 6, 1522
Out of five ships,
        the *Victoria* survives.
        Sebastian del Cano captained her
across the Indian Ocean,
        around the Cape of Good Hope
        along the coast of Africa.
Now eighteen men sail into the harbor:
the first to circle the entire world,
        by the grace of God
        and
        for His glory!

Francisco Pizarro

The Incas called themselves Children of the Sun. Desperate to save their king, they stripped their temples and homes of gold they used to honor the Sun, the source of life.

To Meet the Ransom
Different voices overheard throughout the Inca Empire: 1532

Here at the hitching post of the Sun
where Heaven meets Earth and they are one
we pray Atahualpa's freedom will be won.
Gold. We must get enough gold.
    at Machu Picchu

        This garden graced with golden flowers
        was meant to please the Sun for hours
        and to delight celestial powers.
        Gold. We must get enough gold.
            at Cusco (an official's home)

Gold covers the walls of the Emperor's hall:
Shining hymns to the Sun from dawn to nightfall.
Why must the men with guns have it all?
Gold. We must get enough gold.
    at Cusco (the palace courtyard)

        They must want to lure the Sun away.
        Why else would they want so much gold, I say?
        They hold Atahualpa, and we must pay.
        Gold. We must get enough gold.
            at Tumbes (a merchant's house)

Sir Francis Drake

In 1577 Queen Elizabeth equipped one of her favorites, Francis Drake, with five ships and 164 men to circumnavigate the world. He returned to England with 59 men and two ships. However, he brought a fortune in gold and other treasure, plundered from Spanish and Portuguese caravels.

Remarks to Sir Francis Drake
Queen Elizabeth: aboard the *Golden Hinde*, September 26, 1580

The King of Spain complains to me
of brigandage and piracy.
As I've told his Ambassador,
"It's very risky to explore.
Our sailors have met perils, too.
My tears fall for your King and you."

The King of Spain roils in pain
at the mention of your name.
He says We should cut off your head,
But We've a different plan instead:
A different way to use a sword
to show our love and to reward
your service to the royal crown.

Upon this day as you kneel down,
We hereby knight Sir Francis Drake.
We don't mistake him for a rake.
A heart of solid gold is seen,
as worthy treasure by your queen.

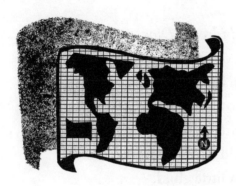

Catalina de Erauso

Abandoned in a convent as a little child, Catalina was on the verge of having to take her final vows. Unexpectedly, she had a chance to escape.

A Prayer in Flight

Catalina de Erauso, outside the convent door: exact location
unknown, 1600

Santa María, Madre de Dios,
Hail Mary, full of grace.
No lack of love for your Son or you
made me wish to leave this place.
The convent with its walls of stone
is the only world that I have known.
Placed here as a little child,
the choice was not my own.
Santa María, Madre de Dios,
please hear the prayer I say.
Santa María, Mother of God,
forgive me for running away.
Intervene, please, with your Son,
so He'll forgive the sins I've done:
the stolen scissors, needle, thread
to do work that might cost my head.

My modest robes
    I'll cut
  then sew . . .
into *men's* clothes—
     a crime, I know.
Yet my heart tells me I must go.
Are not false vows a blasphemy?
Santa María, take pity on me!
Help your hapless servant flee.
Locked up behind the convent door,
I've never seen these streets before.
Inside the world was oh so small.
The outside world—I heard it call—
to beckon me beyond the wall.
Now all alone on this dark night
     Which way?
         Which way?
Run left?
             Run right?
Hail Mary, Mother of Grace.
Help me find a hiding place.

Henry Hudson

Abuchuck Pritckett, one of four survivors of Hudson's last voyage, is on trial for mutiny. This is what he tells the judge.

Mutiny: The Ballad of Henry Hudson
Abuchuck Pritckett: The Swan Publick House, England, 1611

When Henry Hudson first set sail,
    what was his intent?
To find a North Pole Passage
    to the spice-rich Orient.
He sailed to high north latitudes
    beyond 80 degrees,
expecting arctic summer,
    not the biting arctic freeze.
Some sailors, homesick for their wives,
    or maybe just sick of the cold,
      or even just tired
        or risking their lives,
grew cantankerous and bold.

Take a ragtag, bobtail motley crew—
A flotilla of icebergs at sea.
Stir scurvy and hunger into the brew.
You'll be looking at mutiny.

Hudson did what any sane man would do:

He turned toward home and calmed that crew.
The next year Hudson sailed again,
         but the arctic ice prevailed.
With no better luck and no better men
         back home again he sailed.
When the British made no offers,
         Hudson sailed Northeast for the Dutch.
He sailed west when the crew grew skittish,
         a choice the men liked very much.
We sang as we crossed the Atlantic
         in our worthy ship, the *Half Moon*,
Hudson found a grand harbor and river.
         The Dutch were fur traders soon.

England was less than delighted.
Hudson was told, *"Nevermore,*
         can you sail for a foreign country
         and under its flag . . . explore.
         Under England's flag or no flag at all
         can you ever return to the sea . . ."
And with those words the trap was set
         to seal Hudson's destiny.

British traders kept on yearning
         for a short-cut to the East.
They turned to Henry Hudson,
         so he had a chance, at least.
Once again, he headed North,

the route he believed to be best.
But pack ice locked us in Hudson Bay
        with no way out, no getaway. . . .
For eight months the *Discovery*
        was in the grip of the frozen sea.
Then when at last the ship was free
        frustration turned to . . .
                mutiny!
Captain Hudson,
        his son,
                the sick and the lame
        forced into an open boat.
                The carpenter boarded
        by his own choice
before it was set afloat.
No food, no arms, what chance had they
        once
                the *Discovery*
                        sailed away?

And there was nothing I could do.
        And there was nothing I could say.
The mutineers would have doomed me, too,
        in the very same ruthless way.

Take a ragtag, bobtail motley crew—
A flotilla of icebergs at sea.
Stir scurvy and hunger into the brew.
You'll be looking at mutiny.

Samuel de Champlain

The explorer-geographer, who founded the trading post that became the city of Quebec, made repeated trips to France to plead for support of his projects.

Presenting the Case for New France to the Court
Samuel de Champlain, Lieutenant to the
Viceroy of New France: 1615

What a future is just waiting,
just waiting in New France,
if His Majesty
would make a stake,
if the Crown would take a chance.
Costs are high, but may I say
the beauty of this plan
is it will pay its own way.
Rest assured, it can:
      Ancient stands of timber
      and boundless pelts of fur
      are ready for a harvest
      that quickly will defer
      costs of the Crown's investment.

      This far-reaching proposition
would put France in a fine position.

The lakes of North America
        are so huge it seems to me
the chance is great they will connect
        New France to the Western sea!
Imagine, if I find that route across the continent!
        Your ships could sail from sea to sea.
        That is my first intent.
        But . . .
        imagine when France *owns* that route
           and can charge each foreign ship
               a handsome continental toll
                  for every single trip!
I do my best to serve you.
If you'll put me to the test
I might find the Western ocean.
Invest, dear King. Invest!

50

Maria Sibylla Merian

African slaves and East Indians did all the chores in the Dutch colony. An independent, professional woman would have amazed her gardener.

The Lady Who Works
Ravi Bavishi, gardener: Paramaribo, Suriname, 1700

I have not seen a European woman like her.
She does not have slaves
running here,
      running there,
waiting on her for every trifle.
Only when she slips
      into the forest
by canoe,
      going where no Europeans go—
and certainly none of *their* women—
      does she depend on others.
She dresses all by herself, as we do,
      nor does she lazy about,
complaining of "the unbearable heat."
At dawn Madame Merian drinks her tea
and soon is at work
      with pens and paints.
I have never seen such artistry.
Perhaps the gods have touched her,
      giving her a portion

of their powers to create.
Truly, I would not be surprised
    if some day,
one of Madame Merian's butterflies
    flew off the page
and into the garden
    fluttering
        on a passion flower.
    Yes!
    And I would catch it in the net
        with which she has provided me!

Jeanne Baret

The first woman known to have sailed around the world—there may have been unidentified others—did so disguised as a man. What was she really like?

The Botanist's Assistant
M. Jean Baret: the South Seas, 1768

J'étais une fille bien elevée.
A well-brought-up girl was I.
But just being *une fille*
was not my cup of tea.
Adventure was passing me by.
What a waste of a day
 to just sit and crochet.
The memory makes me cry.
But a well-brought-up *fille*
could not go climb a tree
nor explore
like a well-brought-up guy.
Although I learned to play
in a ladylike way
the pianoforte
and the lute,
I was dying to try
a French horn like a guy,
but *une jeune fille*
may not give a toot.

Mama was afraid
I'd end up an old maid.
I needed some ladylike skill.
She said, "Dear, learn to paint."
My reply made her faint.
"*Oui, Mama!*" I cried. "Yes, I will!"
Somehow I just knew
as I sketched and I drew.
Mama had delivered a key.
Wearing young brother's pants,
I said, "*Au revoir, France!*"
and set sail for a new life at sea.

No one bats an eye.
I'm just some shy guy
on Bougainville's grand expedition.
Good work fills my hours:
I paint ferns and flowers,
What bliss to fulfill my ambition!

James Cook

After sending his astronomical observations of an eclipse to the British Royal Society, Cook was given command of a voyage to observe the transit of Venus from Tahiti, and allowed to choose a ship for the expedition. Cook managed to chart New Zealand and to discover Australia on the way home.

Overheard on the *Endeavor*
Commander James Cook: 1768–1771

I first worked on Whitby colliers,
hauling coal in the North Sea.
The virtues of this spacious craft
were not lost on me:
I like its strength,
its flat-bottomed hull,
but what I like the most
is the ease
      of
        steering it
      along
   a
      shallow
coast.
Let others choose ships for grace and for speed.
In unknown waters I know what I need:
a dependable boat,
a boat steady at sea,

a Whitby collier
is the best boat for me.

A wealthy member of the Royal Society, Joseph Banks, brought a retinue of servants and "scientifics" aboard the Endeavor *at his own expense to record the plants and animals they saw. Parkinson made over 1,000 sketches, including the first drawing of a kangaroo.*

Sydney Parkinson, artist: Tahiti, May 20, 1769

As fast as I paint the colors on,
they are swiftly put upon.
Tahitian flies devour them,
then I must start to paint again.
The best scheme that's been devised yet
is to cover my drawings and me with a net.
If I'm painting a fish
          inside such a tent,
the vermin squirm in discontent.
Somehow they manage to get in
and eat up the colors,
so again . . . I begin . . . .

Green was the assistant to the Astronomer Royal.

Charles Green, astronomer: June 3, 1769

When Halley observed Venus
a century ago,

he thought if measurements were made
there would be much to know.
With charts and calculations,
the task is not easily done.
I record my observations,
while the planet crosses the sun.

To an appreciative crew member, an important achievement of the voyage may have been that, for once, nobody died of scurvy.

Charles K. Biggs, seaman: July 12, 1771

At last we're back in England.
Soon the whole world will find out,
Captain Cook has vanquished scurvy
with citrus syrup and . . .
sauerkraut!

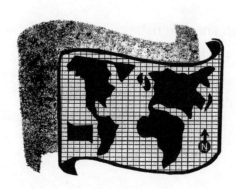

Jean Baptiste Pointe du Sable

Imagine what it may have been like to grow up on a trading post started by your French-Haitian father and Potawatomi mother.

At Our Trading Post
Louis du Sable: Chicago (Eschikagou), 1780

Cinnamon Lou, that's what Papa calls me,
since way back when I was two or three,
before I knew cinnamon was something nice:
rare and tasty, cinnamon spice.
Woodsmen come here to get supplies.
One carved me a toy for an Easter surprise.
The hunters bring their fur pelts here:
moose, mink, otter, beaver, deer . . .
brown bear, black bear, wolverine . . .
and those aren't all the skins I've seen.

Like the French and English do,
Potawatomi trade here, too,
and people like me—
        from all three races—
with a hint of cinnamon
in their faces.

Mary Ann Parker

This sea captain's widow wrote the first known description of Australia.

━ ━ ━ ━ ━ ＾ ━ ━ ━ ━ ━

Notes from *A Voyage Round the World for the Advantage of a Numerous Family*
Mary Ann Parker, widow: England, 1795

There's so much of interest in New South Wales.
I've set down true and lively tales,
of things I had not known before
I sailed on the *Gorgon* Man of War.
My husband, captain of the ship,
invited me to take the trip,
which gifted me with memories.
Herewith I'll share a few of these.

On Captain Parker's passenger list:
    David Burton, the botanist,
    dispatched, just as one would expect,
    to find new plants he should collect;
    Philip King and his pleasant wife
    were off to New South Wales for life;
    He'd start as second in command
    to the governor of that distant land.
    A corps of soldiers was on its way
    to relieve marines at Botany Bay;

a chaplain I found less than charming,
        thirty-one convicts, skilled in farming,
        servants and agents, and the crew.
        For people, I think, that will do.
        (But sixty-six sheep
        should not be ignored
        nor pigs, cows, and fowl,
        which were also aboard.
        They made such a stench
        and raised such a din,
        that a truthful account
        surely must leave them in.)

At the equator, what a surprise
to see this tradition with my own eyes:
Rank and rules are tossed aside
        for this portion of the ride.
Prepared for such a situation
        by a boisterous education,
all laughing with hilarity,
        singing, drinking, merrily,
Captain Parker and his men
        dousing each other
again . . .
        and again
with pails of salt water from the sea!
Young boys at play, they seemed to me.

Sailing toward the Cape of Good Hope,
        we met parties of soldiers
                on their way
                to regroup at Simon's Bay
                and from their to Batavia
to take action
        against the Malays of Java,
who stood accused of poisoning the water.
"The Malays, aren't they taken to be slaves?"
        I asked.
Learning that they were,
I wondered what I might do,
unarmed and faced with such a fate.

The *Gorgon* is a brave and sturdy ship,
It took us through huge swells and squalls,
        past whales and penguins,
slipping between icebergs,
which loomed on every side,
and finally left us safely at our destination.
The governor came aboard for breakfast.
He treated us with such courtesy.
We were shown about the land,
and one day went to Sidney Cove,
We saw natives in canoes,
        We ate parts of kangaroos,
            We saw flightless big emus;
                If greyhounds raced them, they might lose!

But of all the local delicacies,
        what tasted best
were oysters our sailors gathered,
placed round their hats for lack of plates,
then served to us raw and fresh.
        Delicious, simply delicious!

There are many good harbors
that should attract settlers,
but most do not come by choice.
A convict ship arrives from England.
On every side on every bed,
lay the dying and the dead.
To England it matters not a jot
if prisoners arrive alive . . .
        or not.
How many survive?
One in three.
That's the figure given to me.

We sailed for England on December 18,
        having exchanged our soldiers
for marines and their families,
our livestock
        for a menagerie of kangaroos
   and other curiosities,
while our botanist beamed at plants of all varieties.

We stopped in Capetown,
where I bought sixteen canaries in a cage
and gaudy ostrich feathers at a very low price.
On April 6, we arrived in England.
Within a week, I gave birth to a baby boy.

Sacagawea: The Lewis and Clark Expedition (1803–1806)

After the Louisiana Purchase, President Jefferson charged Meriwether Lewis, and, later, William Clark, with crossing the continent and making wide-ranging observations. Jefferson's foremost hope was that the expedition would find a waterway to the Pacific Ocean. As Lewis and Clark assembled the Corps of Discovery, they hired a French-Canadian fur trader as an interpreter because his pregnant wife was from a Rocky Mountain tribe, the Shoshone. And the Shoshone had horses.

Lullaby for Jean Baptiste
Sacagawea: Fort Mandan, March 1805

Hah, hah.
Grow strong, my little one.
Life is a voyage.
Soon you will see.
What will you do?
Who will you be?
Will you be a Shoshone
like me, hah,
like me?

It's been so long,
since I've seen my people,
not since the Hidatsas kidnapped me.
Oh, how I long to be with Shoshone.
To speak and to hear

the words of Shoshone:
the words of the brothers,
the fathers, the mothers,
the words of the People,
the People like me.

Someday,
Hah!
Someday, my little one,
will *you* be
a Shoshone
like me . . . like me?
Will you be a Shoshone
like me?
Hah! Hah!
Will *you* be a Shoshone?
Will you be a *Shoshone*
like me . . . like me?

York: The Lewis and Clark Expedition

Meriwether Lewis did not even list William Clark's slave, York, as a member of the Corps of Discovery. While other participants, even the translator, George Drouillard, were given land grants or good jobs, York was not given his freedom. Clark even refused to hire him out to work in Louisville, where he could see his wife and children.

Explaining to Drouillard
York: Fort Clatsop, Astoria, Oregon, December 11, 1805

My family, we are slaves.
And the Clarks, they are free.
Like his papa was to my papa,
Captain Clark was to me:
First a playmate,
     next a friend,
         but my master
            in the end.
Once boyhood games were set aside,
Young Master's lash could bite my hide.
What Young Master wished,
Young Master did.
As for me,
I did as York was bid.

What was there
I could do or say?
Black slave/White master
It's been that way.
For slaves, no choosing.
Slaves *have* to do.
William Clark joined the army,
I went along, too.

Now he leads the Corps of Discovery.
It's the best thing
that's ever
happened to me.
I've poled the keelboat.
I've paddled the canoe.
But these white men
pole and paddle, too.
When I go hungry,
so do they.
I've never seen
life lived this way.
We carry. We haul
through heat and rain.
I try my best.
I don't complain.
I've had many a chance
to just slip away.
Why don't I do it?
What can I say?

The Captains,
        you men,
        Sacagawea and me,
we've become some sort
        of a company—
something—but not quite—
        a family!
In my heart I am sure
Clark will set me free.
We'll return
and you'll see:
Clark will set me free.
We'll return.
Clark will set me free!

Mary Anning

Just a girl of twelve, Mary knew she made an important find!

Discovery!
Mary Anning: Lyme Regis, England, 1811

I think about my father,
      when I walk
    along the sea.
        It's as if he's talking
and showing things
      to me,
just the way he taught us
to spot a fossil where
    others only see
       some sand
with naught
      of interest there.

That day as I wandered
      beneath the Black Ven cliff,
when I saw that giant fossil
     it almost was as if
Father had said, "Mary,
why do you suppose
     God gave you
  a pair of eyes

to wear
above your nose?"
The fossil was *enormous.*
Was it something from the sea?
I rushed to town to get some men to dig it out for me.
Carefully, so carefully,
removing all debris,
Carefully, so carefully,
I set the skeleton free.
An ancient ichthyosaurus—
a sea reptile that could fly.
Think of giant crocodiles
sailing through the sky!
A neighbor bought the fossil.
Mother was so glad
to add that lovely money
to the little that she had.
Our family celebrated
with tasty treats at tea.
Mother said that Father
would have been quite proud
of me.

John Ross and James Clark Ross

A Polar Inuit recalls the arrival of the Ross expedition and especially John Ross's steamship, Victory. *At the time, this group of Inuit had been cut off from all other civilization for many years.*

The Amazing Surprise
Aviaq, a Polar Inuit woman: Boothia Peninsula, North Arctic, 1829

A whole island of wood,
it moved along,
yes, moved along the sea.
As if on wings
it moved along
as strange as some strange beast might be.
In its depths were many rooms
full of noisy men.
Men in rooms,
and oh, what noise
they kept making again and again.
Little boats hung on the big ship's rail
and the noisy men climbed in.
Down
down
down
they lowered
the boats
while those noisy ones kept up their din.

71

Into the water the little boats went.
Surrounding the ship were they.
"Husband," I said,
"does it not seem
that a monster gives birth today?"
Surrounding the ship like living young,
little boats bobbed in the sea,
as if a monster had given birth.
That's what it looked like to me.

Charles Darwin

Newly graduated as a clergyman, Darwin was eager to be the unpaid naturalist on an expedition to the southern hemisphere and to help the captain find scientific proof that the details of the Book of Genesis were correct.

Journal Jottings
Charles Darwin: 1831–1836

North of Rio de Janeiro, Brazil:
Deep in the tropical forest
a universal silence seems to reign.
Twiners entwining twiners—tresses like hair—
beautiful lepidoptera—
Delight is a weak word to describe what I feel.
I am as a blind man newly given sight.

Punta Alta, Argentina:
There is nothing like geology!
The pleasure of the first day's partridge shooting pales
compared to finding a group of fossil bones,
which tell their story of former times
with almost a living tongue . . . .
Below a high bank in a thick covering of seashells—
a perfect catacomb for monsters of extinct races—
immense bones of truly wonderful size came to light.
Could it be that Creation is more than the work of a week?

The Galapagos Islands, Ecuador:
Such strange creatures!
Huge tortoises, big enough for me to ride;
marine iguanas, dragons dressed in courting colors;
land iguanas, such mild, torpid monsters;
and birds quite fearless and innocent of danger.
What amazes me most are the tiny finches.
Each island's finches have different beaks!
Here both in space and time,
we seem to be brought near to that great fact:
that mystery of mysteries,
the first appearance of new beings on this earth.

Richard Spruce

Botany, like geology, was not considered a "serious science" by the Victorians, but Spruce's work was meticulous.

I Love My Work
Richard Spruce: near Pará, the Amazon Basin, 1850

I'm behaving.
Yes, behaving,
like a proper botanist.
I add species, brand-new species,
to an ever growing list.
Yes, before I laid eyes on them
and made sure that they were listed
no one knew
(and no one cared)
that such plants and trees existed.
I am being,
yes, I'm being,
very, very organized.
Each new day brings new surprises.
Each surprise is super-sized.
Violets are as big as apples.
Daisies bloom on tropic trees.
I'm bamboozled by the bamboo.
How can grasses grow like these?

Just when I say,
"There is no way
I will find one species more,"
my eyes fall on an example
which they've never seen before.
While annoyed by the mosquitoes,
I am blissful,
I insist,
being—
simply being—
a most proper botanist.

Sir John Franklin

Evidence to the contrary, Lady Jane Franklin continued to petition the American president, among others, to help fund search expeditions to find her husband. In 1860 the Royal Geographical Society made her the first woman to receive its gold medal.

Please, Find Sir John!
Lady Jane Franklin speaks to the captain
of another search expedition: London, 1853

"I'll find the Northwest Passage.
I'm certain that I can.
I know those high north waters
as well as any man.
My ship is sound and worthy.
I've picked a splendid crew.
I'll find the Northwest Passage
for England, dear, and you!"
So said Sir John, my husband,
before he sailed away.
Months followed months.
Years followed years.
Each day I wait and pray.
Please find my dearest husband.
God bless your expedition.
Captain, may it be His will
to guide you in this mission.

Give this note to my Sir John,
when you find him, Captain, please.
Now my hopes all rest with you.
Bring him back from Arctic seas.

Ida Pfeiffer

This travel writer never admitted to being frightened, exhausted, or incompetent. Whether a Pacific hurricane was lashing her ship, or she was surrounded by cannibals in Sumatra—or tigers in India—even if she was (temporarily) jailed, Ida always felt "confident and resigned."

A Brief Autobiography
Ida Pfeiffer from a jail cell: Madagascar, 1856

My father so wanted a son
he insisted I be dressed as one.
As soon as Dad died
petticoats were supplied,
but what Mother called "damage" was done.

With my choice of a husband ignored,
Mother found one, but oh, was I bored!
When dear mother expired,
I did what I desired:
I've explored and explored and explored.

I've seen pyramids, jungles, and more.
I've seen churches and mosques by the score.
I've been robbed. I've been swindled,
but my zest has not dwindled.
While there's something to see, I'll explore.

I wonder what Father would say,
if he saw all his children today.
My eight brothers lead lives
drab and dull as their wives.
I live my life a quite different way.

Sir Samuel and Mrs. Florence Barbara Maria Finnian von Sass Baker

On the Bakers' return from Africa in 1865, the Royal Geographical Society awarded Samuel its gold medal and Queen Victoria knighted him.

Two Conversations in London, 1865

Sir Samuel to Lord Babbington:

I was traveling in Hungary
where it's jolly to hunt boar,
when I came upon an ugly scene
that I could not ignore.
A slave market was in progress.
A lovely maid of gentle birth
was being sold at auction:
"This wench, what is she worth?"
A turbaned Turk made the high bid.
Was that young maid to go
to become a sultan's plaything
in some dim seraglio?
Pity quickly turned to love,
which gushed into my heart.
I would make that maid my wife.
We would *never* part!
I outbid that wretched Turk,
then swept my love away.

And not a moment of regret
have I had since that day.
She's admirably adapted
for African exploring:
always uncomplaining
and *never ever* boring.

While Sir Sam was the toast of London, the Queen refused to receive his second wife.

Mrs. Baker to the family cook:

When you explore in Africa
and tent along the Nile,
you won't fuss about the menu.
Food alone will make you smile.
Yes, at times I did the cooking,
so I know how it is done.
One day I poached a hippo,
a rather aged one.
I can't say it was tender,
but Sir Sam did not complain.
He chewed and chewed and chewed and chewed,
then drowned it in champagne.

Sir Sam's my dearest darling,
the hero of my life.
Now all of London fetes him

while ignoring me, his wife.
Because I so adore him,
I stay at home, content
with memories of Africa:
a starry night,
      a tent . . . .

Doctor David Livingstone and Henry M. Stanley

Nothing had been heard from the famous Doctor Livingstone: physician, missionary, anti-slavery spokesman, explorer, and letter writer. Had he been killed, as rumored? Sparing no expense, The New York Herald *gave reporter Henry Stanley a juicy assignment: find Livingstone.*

Two Voices Heard on the Dark Continent
Ujiji, Lake Tanganyika, Africa, October 28, 1871

Livingstone:

The map of Africa was blank,
or very nearly so.
When a place is quite unknown,
that's where I want to go.
So I trekked to Bechuanaland
and took a look around.
The Zuga River, Lake Ngami—
those are what I found.
Next came a discovery—
my how that did please me—
Victoria Falls on the River Zambezi!
Africans call the falls,
"smoke that thunders."
Unseen before by English eyes,
I saw them as God's wonders.

That was thirty years ago.
Now for quite a while,
I've been searching,
    ever searching,
        for the source of the fabled Nile.

Stanley:

I'm just a reporter.
As yet few know my name.
I am looking for a hero.
When I find him, I'll find fame.
I've risked my life to do so,
having left Zanzibar.
This tropic heat is deadly.
What looks near can be far.
I understand this wretched land
might be a man's doom. . . .
Good grief!
    Can it be?
"Dr. Livingstone, I presume?"

John Wesley Powell

Fred Dellenbaugh, age seventeen, could hardly believe his luck when "the Major" accepted him as a member of his second expedition on the Colorado.

The Grand Canyon
Fred Dellenbaugh: the Colorado River, August 22, 1872

The higher the river the faster the ride,
and the waters are high this year.
Our boats whiz along like speeding trains
so fast there's no time for fear.
We'll come to a stretch of lovely calm,
but right around the bend
is a stretch of roaring rapids,
and each one might be our end.
The Major calls them busters
and bust our boats they do.
They lift them up and toss them down.
Then rocks drive holes clean through!
We start to bail and stop to row.
The river rushes in.
Again we cheat disaster.
Death loses its chance to win.
Passing a granite cavern,
we take shelter for the night;
repair the boats as best we can;
set off by dawn's dim light.

We are passing through the canyons,
hemmed in by high stone walls,
dropping deep into the earth
by descending waterfalls.
There's a frenzy of wild waters
that's as fierce as any beast.
Then the Little Colorado
meets the river from the east.
Before us is a vista
freshly fashioned by God's hand.
It's "the knockout punch" of canyons!
No wonder it's called "Grand!"

Charles Wyville Thomson

The repetitive, exhausting work of the first expedition to study the oceans of the world fell to sailors like John Whitcomb. They provided the raw material used to establish a new science: oceanography.

The Challenger Expedition
John Whitcomb: a seaman's complaint, at sea, 1875

How deep? How cold? What lives there?
It's dredge. It's measure. It's trawl.
Samples and more bloody samples.
"Heave away, sailors. Haul!"

It's dredge. It's measure. It's trawl.
This routine—I'm sick of it all.
"Heave away, sailors. Haul!"
Over and over in place after place.

This routine, I'm sick of it all.
Testing the sea. What's in it for me?
Over and over in place after place.
Those scientists and their questions.

Testing the sea. What's in it for me?
Samples and more bloody samples.
Those scientists and their questions.
How deep? How cold? What lives there?

Mary Kingsley

A self-educated child, Mary read books about Africa and set her heart on exploring there.

West Africa Notes
Mary Kingsley: 1893 and 1895

Preparing to Leave, London, July 24, 1893

I'm planning to go as a trader
with fishhooks, toothbrushes, and beads.
A villager won't eat a stranger,
who's bringing him things that he needs.
As a trader I'll make observations
and have a good reason to stay.
Instead of just asking rude questions,
trade seems like a much better way.
I won't travel around with tins of food,
native porters, a stove, and a bed.
I'll eat the food that the villagers eat.
I'll sleep as they do, instead.
I'm hoping the African trusts me
and opens the door to his life.
Or will he think
I'm one more pesty preacher,
who says he should have just one wife?
Thick black skirts and long-sleeved shirts

join high boots in my portmanteau.
The equator is hot. London is not.
Yet that's how I think I should go.

A Coastal Lagoon, October 1893

From the deck of a steamer,
it might be fun
to see crocodiles snoozing
in the African sun.
But if you're trapped by the tide
in a swampy lagoon,
a croc could ruin your afternoon.
If you're in a small boat
and a croc comes to call,
you'll swiftly decide it is not fun at all.
If he climbs in your boat
clip him right on the snout,
or you'll be the one,
who won't be climbing out.
For crocodiles can,
and crocodiles do,
grab at a person in a dugout canoe.

Fang Village, October 1895

It can talk as well as the human tongue:
the tom-tom.
It can make you dance
or want to fight:
the tom-tom.
There is nothing better,
it seems to me,
to reach the soul
of humanity,
than the thrum, thrum, thrum
of the African drum:
the tom-tom.

Fridtjof Nansen

Crossing Greenland, Nansen saw the boats and sleds built by Inuit from driftwood. That convinced him that the Arctic was a frozen ocean with its own currents, which would carry a properly designed boat to the North Pole.

Drifting

Fridtjof Nansen: on the *Fram*, the Arctic, August 1894

Every night I am at home in my dreams,
but when the morning breaks,
         I must gallop back,
           back to the realm of eternal ice.

A summer day, 81 degrees north latitude.
It is lovely, a poem of clear white sunbeams
refracted in the cool crystal blue of the ice,
so wonderfully calm and still.
Not a sound to be heard
     but the drip,
       drip,
     drip
of water from a block of ice
or the dull thud
     of a snow-slip
  from
some hummock.
My thoughts fly free and far

in the profound peace
of the arctic solitude.
Surely the drift
    will become faster and faster,
as we get farther Northwest.
Why should not this winter
    carry the *Fram*
        to someplace north,
    north of Franz Josef Land?
Then off I'd fly
    with dogs and sledges
            to the point where the earth's axis ends.
And the whole
    would go
like a dance!

Margaret Fontaine

This very romantic Victorian woman is always in a tizzy about one man or another, but her love of butterflies lasts a lifetime.

Butterfly Days: Netting
Margaret Fontaine: Damascus, Syria, 1901

My butterfly net
    helps me
        to forget
all sad disappointments
    and   woes.
How could I feel forlorn . . .
    on a bright . . .
sunny . . .
    . . . morn
    while Red Admirals . . .
        flutter . . . above?
With a Camberwell Beauty,
    strong . . .
on the wing,
    who gives
        a fig
        about . . .
                love?
Butterflies are like me:
They yearn to be free

amidst the sun's warmth . . . and the   flowers.
I feel pangs of remorse,
          but keep netting
               (of course!)
                    for hours and hours and   hours . . . .
How could I sigh . . . and . . . moan
                                        as I net a Brimstone
          or I see . . .
               Greater Tortoiseshells
                         flitter.
          After butterfly days
filled with
          splendid
                                             displays,
how could my heart be bitter?

By donkey,
     by horse,
by bicycle,
     (of course!)
with freedom the crown of my life,
     oh, glorious world
with your beauties
     to see
why should I stay home
     as a wife?

Mary Hall

The first woman to cross Africa from the South to the North did so unarmed and unaccompanied by any other Europeans.

Advice to a Missionary's Wife
Mary Hall: Capetown, South Africa, 1905

Travel is a simple matter
if you do as I do, dear.
First, take each and all precautions.
Next, abandon every fear.
When you ford a river,
just wear your mackintosh.
That way your clothing will stay dry,
while your body gets a wash.
Don't forget to bring a hammock.
And no matter what you do,
be fair and friendly with the natives.
They'll be the same with you.

Annie Peck

The Quechua villagers of the Peruvian Andes had seen the diminutive Miss Peck try to summit their perilous mountain before. It's easy to imagine their various comments as she leaves again.

Buena Suerte, Señorita Peck (Good Luck, Miss Peck)
Villagers of Yungay: Peru, 1908

Probrecita, señorita!
                    Pequeñita, Annie Peck!

Can she scale our twin-peaked mountain?

We pray she won't break her neck!

                    Estámos miedosas!
                    There are jutting precipices!

                              Every step is dangerous.
                              What will happen if she misses?

          She must cross a giant glacier.
          before she can reach the top.
                                        She's had frostbite.

She's had blisters.

Nothing seems to make her stop.

She has dressed in triple layers
to protect her from the cold.

    There's a moustache on her ski mask.
    Did she see it? Was she told?

Let us pray to Pachamama:
              Mother Earth, protect our friend.
La pequeñita señorita,
              Let her come to a safe end!

Matthew Henson and Robert Peary

In 1885 Robert Peary hired young Matthew Henson as a servant. Henson, however, became Peary's indispensable partner in reaching the North Pole, where Henson planted a flag.

The Dash to the North Pole
Matthew Henson: April 4, 1909

This jaunt is not a cakewalk.
Forty dogs, five sleds, five drivers, including me:
The brothers Oatah and Egingwah, Seegloo and Ooqueah
Ice ridges sixty feet high

Forty dogs, five sleds, five drivers, including me:
And always the cold, getting colder and colder
Ice ridges sixty feet high
And me out on the hunt for fresh meat

And always the cold, getting colder and colder
Our breath freezes to our hoods and furs.
And me out on the hunt for fresh meat
The 70th meridian, our pathway to the Pole

Our breath freezes to our hoods and furs:
The brothers Oatah and Egingwah, Seegloo and Ooqueah
The 70th meridian, our pathway to the Pole
This jaunt is not a cakewalk.

Alice Huyler Ramsey

Meet the first woman to drive across the United States, a feat she accomplished in only forty-two days.

Part I: Answering Reporters before Leaving

Alice Huyler Ramsey: the Maxwell showroom, New York City,
June 9, 1909

"Yes, my husband gave permission."

"No, he doesn't drive a car."

"Yes, of course, I realize
San Francisco's very far."

"No, my baby will not suffer.
Nurse is kind and competent."

"Yes, they've modified my Maxwell."

"No, I don't know what they spent."

"Yes, it has a larger fuel tank:
20 gallons not 14.
There's a rack with two new tires. . . ."

"No, our veils are crepe de chine."

"Yes, the carbide generator
makes illuminating gas . . . ."

"No. I simply press a rubber bulb:
The horn honk-honks.
I pass."

       "Yes. In case of wind or rain,
       the Pantasote top
       is raised to keep us dry and snug
       until the raindrops stop."

"No. We don't plan to change to trousers.
Dusters keep our clothes protected."

       "Yes, I do believe that women
       can deal with the unexpected."

"No. I can change a tire.
That's quite simple to repair."

       "Yes. I'm confident my Maxwell
       is the car to get us there!"

Part II: As the Journey Is Ending
Oakland, California, July 22, 1909

In Oakland waiting for the ferry
to cross the San Francisco Bay,
how I yearn for my husband, my baby.
My eyes which had so long been fixed
on the road
now blink back a tear,
so eager are they to settle
on loved ones,
so eager are they to settle
on home.

Roald Amundsen and Robert Falcon Scott

Robert Falcon Scott of the British Royal Navy was determined to reach the South Pole before Ernest Shackleton, but discovered he was in a race with an accomplished Norwegian, Roald Amundsen.

Two Expeditions on the Way to the South Pole
1911

Captain Scott said,
"Gentlemen don't practice."

> *Respectful of the frozen continent that lay ahead,*
> *Captain Amundsen was carefully planning*
> *every detail.*

On the way to the South Pole,
Captain Scott said,
"Skis are so foreign."
He ordered his men to an ice floe,
watching as they tried to learn.

> *Meanwhile, Captain Amundsen's team*
> *was streaming over the ice-capped snow,*
> *their Norwegian skis sharp and slick.*

On the way to the South Pole,
Captain Scott said,

"Rotten run of weather . . .
surface of the snow appalling."

Captain Amundsen accepted nature,
the biting cold, the howling winds,
as an acrobat accepts the narrow fact
of the perilous high wire.

On the way to the South Pole,
Captain Scott said,
"We'll leave these beasts behind."
Abandoning the huskies,
his weary, half-starved crew
forged on alone in dread,
their code of loyalty surviving trust.

Captain Amundsen's dogs
were his great joy, his "children"—
well-fed and well-loved companions—
dependable partners,
and if necessary, food for survival.

At the South Pole
Captain Scott said nothing.

The flag of Norway rustled in the shining whiteness
The sign that Amundsen had gotten there first.

Ernest Shackleton

Shackleton followed the Norwegian example in preparing for his second expedition to the Antarctic. He considered every detail. To finance the trip, he promised his backers all of the earnings from the book he would write. An Australian photographer would film the voyage.

Voices Heard on the Way South
1914–1917

Preparations: Sir Ernest Shackleton

I received nearly 5,000 applications.
From these I picked fifty-six men.
While we anchored in Margate,
          war clouds darkened.
We had been preparing to explore,
      but now our country
        was edging toward
       a war.
The crew was mustered on the deck.
Along with our ship and stores,
might I offer our services?
All agreed.
Yet when I asked if we could fill some need,
the Admiralty wired back, "Proceed."
"We wish the Expedition to go on,"
said Mr. Winston Churchill.

The King himself handed me the Union Jack.
Midnight of that same day, war was declared.
With clear orders
        we sailed for Buenos Aires
                and from there to South Georgia,
What welcome was the Weddell Sea preparing?

Pack Ice: Frank Worsley

        The Boss calls pack ice nature's jigsaw puzzle,
                large chunks that drift and jam into each other.
        There's peril but not much puzzle
    with the loose-pack,
        which we can steam through.
    The puzzle pieces spread upon the sea is old pack,
        thickened by rafts of young ice.
    We look for leads,
    narrow
open
    lanes
through which we navigate
        with care.
                But don't *ever* count on pack ice to play fair:
big floes can lock together, jamming harder and harder into
close-pack,
        trapping your ship in a sea of ice
            the way a pack of wolves
        might trap a deer.

Photographing: Frank Hurley

Frosted with moonlight,
the ship looks like a Christmas cake tonight.
Here is a moment I'll capture:
the sea white and motionless
holding our ship in its frozen grip.

The Dogs: Frank Wild

I know the Boss has no heart for dogs.
To him they're just necessities,
but not to me: God bless our dogs.
I love their cheerful curiosity,
their enthusiasm for learning and for life.
They try their best to understand.
Some all but talk: God bless our dogs.

Small Wonder: Alexander Macklin, ship's doctor

When at last we reached Elephant Island,
men reeled along the barren beach,
picking up handfuls of stones,
letting them trickle through their fingers
like misers gloating over gold.
Solid land!
    After days at sea

in open boats
with no warm food,
    our clothing worn and wet,
after months of camping on ice floes,
solid land.
    Hurrah! Hurrah! Hurrah!

The Fourth Man: Shackleton

Anxiety for my brave men
then gave me but one thing to do:
get whalers' help to rescue them.
I left Wild in command on Elephant Island.
    In the worn *James Cairn,*
        on a frosty sea,
    four others went for help with me.
    So great were the gales,
        so small our boat,
hardly a spot was dry.
    Three men took turns at the watch:
    one at the tiller ropes,
        one at the sail,
and the third,
    for all he was worth,
        had to bail.
When a gigantic wave deluged the boat, even our cook stove was afloat.
    And nature had more in store before
        the winds and the waves drove us ashore.

As evening fell on the sixteenth day,
    we reached the beach at Haakon Bay.

We slept in a cave that first night.
Morning was clear and cold and bright.
Still the whaling station at Stromness Bay
    lay one hundred and fifty miles away.

Was our party fit for such a trip?
    Was the battered *James Cairn* a seaworthy ship?
The answer was "no," so you'll understand
    why I planned to get there overland.

Upturned, the *James Cairn* made a shelter for three.
Just Crean and Worsley would trek with me.
The carpenter using *James Cairn* screws,
    made ice-gripping boots from my thin-soled shoes.
With provisions for three days,
    fifty feet of alpine rope,
        the three of us left with cautious hope.
                Across a glacier,

    up a slope . . .
At first the full moon was our guide,
    revealing what the snow could hide.
        Then thick fog drifted all around,
hiding the dangers of ice-capped ground.
    We proceeded roped together,
    a precaution in such weather.

Jagged peaks and deep crevasses
    on and over night and day.
At last we glimpsed Husavik Harbor,
      and heard a whistle from the bay.
All our aches and pains forgotten,
we shook hands without a word.
      The whalers' whistle was like music,
the sweetest music ever heard.
We still had to face the challenge
     of a very steep descent,
but we sensed a fourth man with us,
a helpful presence, Heaven sent.
We had seen God in his splendors
. . . heard the text that Nature renders.
We had reached the naked soul of man.

Bessie Coleman and Amelia Earhart

Returning from France after World War I, John Coleman told his sister that in France people of color were accepted as equals and women could become aviators.

My Kid Sister, Bessie
John Coleman: Chicago, July 1937

Turn on your radio.
You'll hear about Amelia sure enough,
how she set off to fly around the world
in a Lockheed Electra,
the latest thing with wings.
The whole country knows Amelia:
that blond girl, slim, smiling, sure of herself.
"Amelia Earhart Disappears . . ."
        "Lady Lindy Lost . . ."
The newspapers are full of Amelia.
But as for me,
I am full of memories,
memories of a colored girl
every bit as brave as Amelia.
A sweet, sassy colored girl.
A smart girl,
pretty . . .
and talk about stubborn!

Nobody and no thing
could turn our Bessie round.
She wasn't out to set world records.
Her dream: to start a school,
a flying school for girls of color,
so they could learn to fly
the way Amelia Earhart learned,
right here in America.

ner . . .

thin-

and even . . .

grows thinner . . .

to where the air

and even . . . higher

higher . . .

they're letting us go

Could that be why

that Hillary is no ordinary guy.

that even, it seems the gods agree

each in such great quantity

determination, decency, strong will—

I see modesty, endurance, and great skill—

he answers "Just an ordinary guy."

When I ask what these strange words mean,

He calls himself "an average bloke."

but none like him.

I have guided others up these steep slopes,

Sir Edmund Hillary and Tenzing Norgay

Summiting

Tenzing Norgay: May 29, 1953

A beekeeper from New Zealand
and me, a sherpa from Nepal,
climbing together over snow and ice
crossing deep crevasses
going higher and higher
getting closer and closer
to the edge of the heavens
the highest place on earth.
Outsiders call it Mt. Everest.
For us it is Chomolungma,
home of the gods: a holy place.

Tenzing Norgay, the guide who summited with Hillary, became his good friend.

Yuri Gagarin

Imagine witnessing the first man about to leave earth for outer space.

Dawn at the Cosmodrome

A man in the crowd: Kazakhstan, Soviet Republic, April 12, 1961

Gleaming behind him,
    the gigantic rocket made Gagarin
look like a toy, a miniature man in orange overalls.
Yet there was nothing small in what he was to do.
A white helmet framed his young face.
"Dear Friends," he said,
"To be the first man in space . . .
    to meet nature face to face—
        could one dream of anything greater?
To be the first to do what generations
    have dreamed of doing,
        to pave the way into space for humanity . . .
what a responsibility . . .
for the present . . .
and for the future."

John Glenn

Glenn and other Project Mercury astronauts made a point of meeting the workers—and not just the engineers—who were building space hardware. Z-D, for zero defects, became a manufacturing motto.

John Glenn, the First American in Orbit

Walter Morris, factory worker: San Diego, California,
February 20, 1962

He shook my hand.
His eyes met mine.
We spoke about the fine design—
    the strength,
        precision,
            rockets need
                to get space capsules
                    up to speed.

On the job I often thought
about John Glenn, the astronaut.
I couldn't let mistakes slip by.
A tiny flaw might kill the guy.
When I heard Glenn would be the first
to orbit earth, I nearly burst.
Each time his mission was delayed,
    my stomach churned.
        I hoped.
            I prayed.

Then finally on the 11th try,
      he catapulted through the sky!
Imagine, giving all your worth
      to blast through space
           and circle Earth?

Valentina Tereshkova

During the space race there were some who thought outer space was just for men.

Valentina Teresh . . . what?

Voices heard at Bill's Barbershop: Austin, Minnesota, June 19, 1962

They sent a dame to outer space?
> *You're kidding me.*
> What a disgrace!
The poor thing will be wrecked for life.
> What man would want her for a wife?
> *Thank goodness in the U.S.A.*
> *we do things in a different way!*
We don't let women do men's work.
> *The man in charge must be a jerk.*
> She orbited *longer* than our guys?
That's got to be a pack of lies!
> *Who but those Commies would have thought*
> *a dame could be . . . an astronaut?*

119

Neil Armstrong, Michael Collins, Edwin (Buzz) Aldrin, Jr.

For years people playfully imagined there was a Man in the Moon. What if they were right?

The Landing
The Man in the Moon: July 20, 1969

Armstrong, Collins, and the one called Buzz—
I'm not alone as once I was.
When human eyes first noticed me,
the moon was sacred, a mystery.
Ancient people bowed before it.
No one since could quite ignore it.
Spooning lovers saw its phases.
Swooning poets sang its praises.
Watching the moon traverse the sky,
     folks saw *me*!
        They saw . . . a guy!
(Except the people in Japan
     who saw a rabbit—
        not a man!)
Now scientists insist my face
is just an illusion, distorted by space.
After yearning to get here for centuries,
Earthlings have done it. They've sent these:
Armstrong, Collins, and the one called Buzz.
I'm not alone as once I was.

Sally Ride

The first American female astronaut describes the feeling of going beyond earth's gravity and into space.

On the Space Shuttle *Discovery*
Sally Ride: June 1983

Strapped in place,
      we check our gear.
Liftoff time is growing near.
The power units start to whir.
      The shuttle starts to shake.
Countdown begins.
Launch engines light.
      In a blazing trail,
        we rise in flight.
          The rockets fall as we streak toward space,
while gravity
      presses
        at such a pace
          it begins to seem
            too much to stand.
Then
      as if a giant lifted his hand,
we're weightless
      and the feeling's . . . grand!

Mae Jemison, MD

The first woman of color to be an astronaut knew what she wanted to do when she was very young.

- - - - - ^ - - - -

A Science Mission Specialist
Mae Jemison, MD: September 1992

"There's nothing that you cannot do."
"There's no one you cannot be."
I proved my parents' words were true.
I lived the lessons they taught me.
A child of the space age,
  beguiled by one thought:
   I want to be an astronaut!
And as I grew I kept my eyes
as the song said to do,
"on the prize . . . on the prize."
First an engineer,
  then a medical degree,
next the Peace Corps
  and Africa hummed to me,
while I held the thread of a young child's thought:
I want to be an astronaut!

Now a scientist in outer space,
I've proved my parents true.
"There's no one who you cannot be."
"There's nothing you cannot do."

122

Heather Halstead

Wilbur was one of many students who was able to travel with Heather Halstead, an innovative young educator, on her sailboat expedition around the word, via the Internet.

New Explorers
Wilbur Torres: Bronx, New York, December 1999

We're in school,
but it feels like we're part of the crew
on the round-the-world trip of the *Makulu II*.
When our class connects to the Internet,
we "Reach the World."
(That's the site we get.)
Then we open the Ship's Log
so that we can share
new sights and insights we find posted there.
We see maps of our route
      so that we understand
         where we're going to sail,
where we (probably) will land.
      We see photos of places.
        We see scads of new faces.
          We see all kinds of cultures.
            We see all the world's races.
If we want to know something—
      this part is the best—
we just e-mail the crew

and make our request.
Then we can find out
    what kids miles away
      study in school
        or what games
          they might play
            or what thoughts
              they might think
                or what food they might eat.
We're exploring the world
In a way that's so neat
that geography beckons
and school . . .
    is a treat.

Dr. Amos Nur and Dr. Jean-Daniel Stanley

Two experts from different fields of science speculate what happened to an ancient city discovered by an underwater archaeologist.

Herakleion: An Underwater City in the Bay of Abukir off the North Coast of Egypt

Dr. Amos Nur and Dr. Jean-Daniel Stanley: December 2000

Dr. Nur, Geologist

Did some cataclysm happen?
Or did the city slowly sink?
Did an underwater landslide
cause an earthquake,
as I think?

Dr. Stanley, Oceanographer

Herakleion stood on marshland,
waterlogged and almost mud.
While I don't rule out an earthquake,
I think there was a flood.

We know an earthquake
toppled Troy.
One toppled Jericho.
Perhaps there's a still-hidden fault
Just where, we still don't know.

125

If there had been an earthquake,
It would seem to me
there would be a record,
but there's none that we can see.

The temple has a long
    deep
      crack:
proof of tectonic force. . . .

That crack is typical of deltas,
of large rivers
changing course. . . .

What happened at Herakleion?
The jury may still be out.
Asking questions, seeking answers . . .
That's what exploring's all about!

Sylvia A. Earle, PhD

A student realizes the parallel between deep-sea oceanographic exploration and outer space.

Sylvia Earle: Deep Ocean Explorer
Lori Faye: Aptos, California, March 29, 2001

Her eyes might gaze
    toward
      distant
        stars,
but not for her the lure of Mars.
She's challenged by a different place,
    just as unknown as outer space.
Not for her the stratosphere
    but a life-filled, liquid atmosphere—
where she can be . . . a pioneer!
    Down,
      down,
        down
          in
the depths of the sea,
    where
      no human
        had gone before.
    Down,
    down,

down
to
the deepest deep —
exploring
the ocean floor.

Spirit and Opportunity

Ever since they landed on opposite sides of Mars, roving robots Spirit and Opportunity have been working as explorers, sending back information and photographs to Earth via Odyssey, an orbiting satellite.

Imagining the Future
2004

Spirit:
Who will future explorers be?
Space orbiters like Odyssey!
And my robots like my mate and me!
I'm Spirit.

Opportunity:
Who will future explorers be?
Space orbiters like Odyssey!
And robots like my mate and me!

I'm Opportunity.

Before we even were designed,
Odyssey circled Mars to find
details of its geography:

Where might traces of water be?

Sending messages to Earth below,
it told NASA what it wished to know.
NASA planned an expedition,
equipping us to do the mission.

NASA planned an expedition,
equipping us to do the mission.

Above the Earth . . .

Beneath the stars . . .
Here we are exploring Mars!

Here we are exploring Mars!

I'm Spirit.

                                    I'm Opportunity.

They call us Rovers,   *They call us Rovers,*
as if we were   *as if we were*
a couple of dogs   *a couple of dogs*
with teeth and fur.   *with teeth and fur.*
                                    Instead of legs,
                                    we have six wheels.

And we don't beg
for snacks or meals.

                                    Nor do we leap

nor do we race.
We keep a slow and steady pace.   *We keep a slow and steady pace.*
With panels powered by the sun,

                                    inch by inch we'll get things done.

Rovers: hounds of the red planet!

                                    Why risk life? Let robots man it.
NASA counts on my mate and me!   *NASA counts on my mate and me!*
I'm Spirit.

                                    I'm Opportunity.

Author's Note

What might we make of the world if we didn't gradually soak up the accumulated knowledge of those who came before us? It's a long stretch from our age of technology to a time before even the idea of geography—recording coastlines, rivers, and mountains on maps and identifying them by name—had occurred to anyone. That long stretch, however, is what this book invites you to make.

It might help to imagine a large globe, the kind you see in a classroom or library. But this globe is blank and colorless. Those invisible lines—the equator, latitude, and longitude— loop around a vast unknown without coastlines or continents. Motivated by trade and curiosity, the earliest explorers traveled beyond the known boundaries of home, gradually acquiring a sense of what was where.

Maps began to appear in Greece early in the fifth century BC. One of them shows a flat disk of land edged with water. The Greek historian Herodotus (484–424 BC) traveled widely himself and carefully listened to other travelers' tales. Herodotus described the world as a sphere, and his descriptions were the basis for the first map that looks somewhat like the world as we know it today. As the most famous Greek explorer and empire builder, Alexander the Great, led his armies beyond any place seen on the maps of his day, he supposedly had specimens of plants and animals collected and sent back to Greece for his teacher, Aristotle. From the very earliest times, even before him, exploration has been linked with science.

The Christian world, however, turned away from almost all of the information that "pagan" explorations had produced, and used the Bible as a scientific text. Once again maps showed a flat Earth. Meanwhile, unhindered by either competition or religious doctrine, the Islamic world cornered trade with the Indies for what had become as precious as jewels: spices. Europeans paid the stiff prices, but how they bristled. Imagine this: pepper, that nearly constant companion of salt now found on almost every dining table, was once so valuable that people would pay their rent with peppercorns!

Add the passion for spices to a new spirit in the fifteenth century. Ancient maps and writings were being rediscovered. The Renaissance, a time of rebirth of art and science (a re-*naissance* in French), gradually was beginning. Herodotus had written that the Phoenicians successfully had sailed around the coast of Africa two thousand years earlier. Yet when Prince Henry the Navigator first created a center of learning about geography and navigation in Portugal, sailing across the equator still was considered impossible. Surely the boiling waters would melt the pitch that held the oakum in place and boats would fall apart! Once Henry's sailors discovered otherwise, the most famous era of exploration . . . and exploitation . . . began.

Backed by the Pope and their respective monarchs, Portugal and Spain proceeded to divide up the "pagan world," saving souls and filling their coffers (and more than a few pockets) as they ravaged one civilization after another. On July 1, 1511, Portugal sent a war squadron to India. In a blow that staggered Islamic trade, Portugal overcame the Sultan of Malacca.

The booty of the Indies was brought to Rome, as well as exotic animals, such as leopards and even an elephant, which supposedly knelt before the Pope. The names of Portuguese and Spanish explorers, *los conquistadores*, the conquerors, are the ones we know best. Soon Holland, England, and France joined the race to build empires by exploration.

The search for a shorter route to the Indies—to spices and riches—led to the "discoveries" of North and South America, as well as the Arctic and Antarctic regions.

The lure of the unknown was irresistible. Even before the United States declared independence, Americans were exploring lands to the West. During the nineteenth century, the focus of Europe was on Africa.

It's neat but not accurate to jump from ancient Greece to the *conquistadores*. The whole world didn't stay at home, waiting for the Renaissance. Vikings in their speedy, seaworthy boats stormed from Scandinavia to raid England and Ireland, where genetic studies now show they carried off Irish and English women along with other treasures. The Vikings settled Iceland and Greenland, and were probably the first Europeans to start a settlement in North America.

From northern Spain Rabbi Benjamin of Tudela traveled throughout Europe and the Middle East, making a survey of the Jewish populations and providing us with a mid-twelfth century social history. Genghis Khan's brilliant horsemen swept across Asia and into Russia. His descendant, the Kublai Khan, engaged Marco Polo, a young trader from Venice, to serve him. When Marco Polo returned to Venice with stories of a fabulous kingdom in the East, nobody believed him. Ibn Battuta, starting in Morocco, where he left for his first trip to Mecca, traveled more than seventy-five thousand miles in the fourteenth century. In China, well before the *conquistadores* and their caravels, Zheng He had created a fleet of sailing ships unequaled in size until the world wars of the twentieth century! Zheng He's ships sailed to India and Africa, and there are some indications that they even reached their destinations. When the Confucians took over the court, Zheng He's fleet was destroyed, as was most of the information about his discoveries of the world outside China.

I'm tempted to use quotes around "discover" and "discoveries" because almost all of the places the explorers explored, with the exception of Antarctica, outer space, and mountaintops such as Everest, were well known to the people who lived there: native people who were discounted by the explorers. Monarchs and governments dispatched expeditions to claim lands inhabited by "pagans and infidels" for their respective countries. It was the rare explorer, such as Charles Darwin, Mary Kingsley, David Livingstone, Matthew Henson, and Sir Edmund Hillary, among others, who respected the cultures of non-Christian people and did not see these people as "savages" or "children," potential converts, and/or slaves: creatures somehow less valuable than anyone from European countries or the United States.

Although I might find much about many explorers politically incorrect and worse, I am in awe of their bravery and endurance. Thomas Jefferson's description of Meriwether Lewis as having "courage undaunted" could surely apply to many explorers. Just imagine. Until the last quarter of the eighteenth century, when the chronometer made it possible to measure longitude, explorers at sea often could only guess at where they were. Islands, in particular, were "discovered and claimed," only to be lost because neither their discoverers nor anyone else could find them again! Small wonder that when Britain was at the height of its power, a prize of ten thousand pounds was offered to whoever could devise a method of accurately determining longitude.

Explorers faced incredible hardships. Added to the dangers of long sea voyages and overland travel through all sorts of terrain from jungle to tortuous ice fields were illnesses: frostbite, typhoid, malaria, fevers, and scurvy, the wasting illness caused by lack of vitamin C that eventually causes death. During the four years that I have been writing these poems, I've been inside replicas of Columbus's caravel, the *Nina*, Henry Hudson's *Half-Moon*, and Sir Francis Drake's *Golden Hind*. They are shockingly small. It's hard to think of being at sea for months and sometimes years on such a ship, packed with people and provisions and live animals held above the decks in slings. The smells must have been horrific. And when I read about the many people who explored the frigid Arctic and Antarctic, I cannot help but be so appreciative, again and again, that I am *reading* about, not living through, these expeditions.

Little by little and then at a gradually quickening rate, our imaginary blank globe was filled in with piece after piece like a huge jigsaw puzzle. As I researched, I kept coming across the phrase, "The Great Age of Exploration." Sometimes it referred to the period of the *conquistadores* during the fifteenth and sixteenth centuries. Sometimes it referred to the nineteenth-century exploration of Africa. When Antarctica was explored, I read that the Great Age of Exploration was over. Try telling that to contemporary explorer/adventurers with an appetite for danger that draws them to the distant and perilous!

I believe the Greatest Age of Exploration is going on right now. Just think! Explorers of the twenty-first century are going not only to the deepest depths of the earth's seas with Sylvia Earle, but to the farthest reaches of space via technology. Robots capable of accomplishing complex tasks where humans could not survive are pushing the boundaries of the possible. The real explorers of today have merged with "scientifics." I call them "explorifics." They are oceanographers, marine biologists and astrobiologists, astrophysicists, engineers, and other highly trained experts, as well as educational innovators like Heather Halstead. It's a very exciting time with lots of opportunities for the brave and determined. Maybe you will be among them.

About the Explorers

Edwin "Buzz" Aldrin, Jr. (1930–)

Born in New Jersey, Aldrin graduated from the United States Military Academy at West Point in 1951 and went on to get a PhD from MIT (Massachusetts Institute of Technology). Like Neil Armstrong, Buzz Aldrin was involved in the Gemini program and spent more than five hours outside the spacecraft during the docking procedure of Gemini 12. However, Aldrin's Gemini achievements almost pale beside the fact that he was one of the three astronauts who left Earth on July 16, 1969, on the Apollo mission. Four days later he became the second human to descend from the lunar module Eagle to what he called "the magnificent desolation" of the moon itself. (Exploring the moon wasn't as much fun as one might guess. It was a challenge to adjust movements to avoid falling, moon dust managed to cling to space suits, and the glare of the sun could cause Aldrin and Armstrong to see their own faces in their helmets.) As Colonel Aldrin, he retired from NASA in 1972 to start an aerospace consulting firm. (See also Neil Armstrong and Michael Collins.)

Alexander the Great (356–323 BC)

Philip II of Macedonia had united the Greek city-states. When he was killed in 336 BC, his twenty-year-old son, Alexander, took over his father's plan to conquer the Persians. In less than two years, Alexander was leading his armies into unmapped lands in Asia Minor. Before he turned toward home, he had explored and conquered not only Persia and Egypt, but lands completely unknown to the Greeks: lands as far west as Libya in Africa and as far east as the Indus River, beyond the modern countries of India and Afghanistan. In the process Alexander founded over seventy cities, including Alexandria in Egypt and Karachi in India. He explored the Indus River, learning that it was not the source of the Nile. Finally, after ten years, he led his army back to Greece. One year later Alexander, just thirty-two years old, died, but not before dispatching two naval expeditions: one to explore the Caspian Sea and another to find an ocean route from the Red Sea to India. The amazing empire did not last long, but signs of Hellenistic culture still mark the lands he conquered.

Roald Amundsen (1872–1928)

Roald Amundsen said that the English explorers he read about as a boy in Norway inspired him to leave medical school and to join the first expedition that wintered on Antarctica. In 1906 he sailed through the legendary Northwest Passage. The British, never at a loss for bravery, had been trying to find it for several hundred years. A protégé of Fridtjof Nansen, Amundsen originally planned to try drifting to the North Pole, as Nansen had. He left Norway in August of 1910 in Nansen's ship, the *Fram*. Meanwhile, Robert Falcon Scott had left for Antarctica in June with great fanfare. Amundsen's crew was surprised and delighted to learn that they were going there, too! Traveling light and wearing traditional Eskimo furs, Amundsen and four men traveled toward the pole with speed. At first they were able to ski over the snow fields strapped to the sledges, but they had to fight their way up treacherous glaciers. Settling into camp on December 13, only fifteen miles from the pole, Amundsen says he felt the "intense expectation" he remembered as a child on Christmas Eve. The next day the Norwegians planted their flag at the bottom of the world. Amundsen went on to navigate the Northeast Passage and fly over the North Pole in a dirigible. He left to search for a missing pilot and disappeared like one of his childhood heroes. (See also Fridtjof Nansen, Robert F. Scott, Ernest Shackleton.)

Mary Anning (1799–1847)

The word "explorers" usually makes us think of people traveling many miles across oceans or deserts. But the woman who would be called "the greatest fossilist of her time" explored a three-mile stretch of narrow beach between rocky cliffs and the sea within walking distance of her home in England. As a child, she had helped her father look for fossils, which he sold. After he died, the family was so poor that Mary had to leave school. She was eleven years old. The money she earned selling fossils was a necessity. At about that time her brother found a skull of what looked like a crocodile's cousin. A year later Mary found the rest of the skeleton. In spite of her lack of formal education, Mary continued to look for fossils and to do her best to learn about them. Mary made impressive discoveries; pterodactyls, plesiosaurs, and icthyosaurs. Over the years, scientists such as Richard Owens, who coined the word "dinosaur," and the geologist William Buckland came to Lyme Regis to go on fossil hunts with Mary.

Neil Armstrong (1930–)

The United States was trailing the Soviet Union in the space race, but President John F. Kennedy convinced Congress that the U.S. could move to first place by putting a man on the moon. Fueled by that vision, American industry, technology, and taxpayer dollars had a goal. After Neil Armstrong had graduated from Purdue University with a degree in aeronautical engineering, he went to work as a test pilot for NACA, the National Advisory Committee on Aviation, which later became NASA. After flying more than two hundred models of aircraft, Neil became an astronaut in 1962. As the command pilot on *Gemini 8*, he was the first civilian ever to command an American space mission. The "first" he will be remembered for, however, will be the step he took on the moon, the step he called "a small step for man, a giant step for mankind." The whole world was watching the *Apollo 11* from takeoff to splashdown. Its three astronauts were honored as heroes. Armstrong stayed with NASA for many years to coordinate its research. Then he headed a company called AIL Systems in Deer Park, New York. (See also Edwin "Buzz" Aldrin, Jr., and Michael Collins.)

Sir Samuel (1821–1893) and Mrs. Florence Barbara Maria Finnian von Sass Baker (1841–1916)

A widower with four children, Sir Samuel Baker was a darling of the British Empire. He had written several books on his adventures in Ceylon and as a hunter. His second wife, however, was a "dubious peccadillo." Was she an orphan of a noble German family? A victim of the Revolutions of 1848? A Hungarian? Younger than his oldest daughter and much prettier, she had a hint of scandal about her. Like other English explorers, the Bakers had searched for the source of the Nile by following its tributaries. They met another explorer, John Speke, who claimed—inaccurately as it was proved—that he had already found the river's source. Changing their destination to Luta Ngize, they were the first Europeans to see the large lake, which they renamed Lake Albert, after the Queen's consort. They found Murchison Falls at the lake's north end. While they helped fill in the map of the area, they also made a report on the slave trade. "Mrs. Baker is not a screamer," said Sir Sam; fevers, dangerous camp mutinies, and lack of food would have given her many opportunities to be one. The Bakers returned to Africa several times and worked for the Egyptian government to stop the slave trade.

Vasco Núñez de Balboa (1475–1519)

Packed in a box marked COMESTIBLES, Balboa escaped his creditors in Hispaniola, on a ship bound for Colombia. The ship was going to save settlers from attacks by natives. Soon Balboa was in command of the settlement, which he moved to Panama. He "married" the daughter of a native chief to get gold, and he set dogs upon the natives to get more. When stories of Balboa's outrageous behavior reached Spain, the king sent word that he was replacing Balboa with Pedrarias d'Avila, a more dependable man from Hispaniola. That prompted Balboa to march one hundred and ninety Spaniards and hundreds of native porters across Panama in search of the "great South Sea." When they reached the Sierra de Quareca Mountains, there were only sixty-seven survivors. Balboa claimed what became known as the Pacific Ocean for Spain. The king made Balboa Adelante of the Mar de Sur, but subject to the authority of d'Avila. Balboa was later convicted of treason and beheaded.

Jeanne Baret (1740?–1803?)

The first French circumnavigation of the world was an expedition under the leadership of Louis-Antoine de Bougainville, after whom the beautiful tropical plants, bougainvillea, were named. After stopping in the Falkland Islands to reclaim them for Spain, the expedition's next mission was to find the "lost continent" Terra Australis. When the ships reached Tahiti, the natives immediately recognized that the botanist's assistant, a very modest young man, Monsieur Jean Baret, was, in fact . . . a young woman! While Philibert Commerson, the botanist, insisted he had no idea that Jean was Jeanne, he asked for permission to stay on Mauritius with her. During the next five years, they collected plants from that island, as well as from Madagascar. When Commerson died, Jeanne carefully organized their collection and sent it to the royal Cabinet d'estampes in France. Natural scientists recognized it as an invaluable contribution, but Commerson received all the credit. Little is known about Baret's early life. Perhaps no one ever asked.

Ibn Battuta (1304–1368?)

When his *Rihla*, or story, was translated in the nineteenth century, European artists as well as explorers were intrigued by the exotic places he had visited. Starting with his first *hajj*, (or pilgrimage) to Mecca, Battuta traveled throughout Dar al Islam, the widespread Muslim world. Battuta went to India and spent seven years in Delhi at the court of the Sultan Mohammed Ibn Tugluq, "whose gate is never without some poor man being enriched, or some living man being executed." Tugluq sent him as his ambassador to China with gifts including "a hundred thoroughbred horses and . . . a hundred white slaves." (By the time Battuta reached the Maldives, bandits had relieved him of his gifts.) He visited the windswept Russian steppes and was honored by "Christian infidels" in the Crimean city of Feodosyia. Staying at a mosque surrounded by churches, he heard a new sound: "bells on every side . . . I bade my companions climb the minaret and chant the Koran." Although he was a strict Sunni Muslim and had studied Muslim law, Battuta often sought guidance from Sufis, Muslim mystics.

Rabbi Benjamin Ben Jonah of Tudela (1127–1173)

Rabbi Benjamin left Tudela in northern Spain, traveling through much of Europe, Africa, and Asia. He was probably the first European to reach China and Tibet. Perhaps his motivation was to help Jews find a safe haven from Crusaders; his record, *The Itinerary of Rabbi Benjamin of Tudela,* inventories and evaluates the Jewish communities in the many places he visits. In this early travel guide, the Rabbi tells how far one location is from

145

the next and often comments on the place's commerce, history, and architecture. Sometimes he retells legends; sometimes he makes colorful observations: pearl fishing on the island of Kish, or how pepper is grown and processed in Kulam. "In Kulam, an African trading center, where both Jews and non-Jews are black, the summer sun is so hot that people light the streets and markets to 'turn night into day.'" Originally written in Hebrew, *The Itinerary* was translated into many languages. It became a resource for Jews forced to leave Spain in 1492.

William Clark (1770–1838)

As Meriwether Lewis began plans for the grand expedition to find a Northwest Passage to the Pacific Ocean, he realized the need for a co-captain to accomplish President Jefferson's goals. Lewis had served in the army under William Clark in an elite company of sharpshooters for just six months, but the men had formed a strong friendship. More skilled at mapmaking and surveying, Clark had skills that complemented Lewis's strengths in the natural sciences. Once the "invitation to greatness" was made, the names "Lewis & Clark" became linked in American history. A tough woodsman, Clark was born in Virginia, but grew up and lived in Kentucky. He had good leadership skills, so while Lewis saw to assembling supplies and having a boat built, Clark started to recruit the "stout, healthy young men . . . accustomed to the woods and capable of bearing . . . fatigue" who would make up the Corps of Discovery. The hardships of the expedition only served to reinforce the trust the two captains had in each other. When at last the expedition returned to a triumphant reception, Lewis insisted that Clark be given equal honor and financial reward, even though Lewis had only been authorized to have a lieutenant—not a captain—as his second officer. Although denying him the position of captain, the Senate confirmed Jefferson's appointment of Clark to be Superintendent of Indian Affairs for Louisiana Territory with the rank of brigadier general. Following Lewis's suicide, Clark eventually had an edited version of their journals published. However, in 1904, some hundred years after Lewis and Clark were crossing the continent, the complete, original journals were published in eight volumes. (See also Meriwether Lewis, Sacagawea, and York.)

Bessie Coleman (1892–1926)

The middle child in a large family, Bessie eagerly learned all she could in a segregated one-room schoolhouse in Texas. Her brothers thought she'd have more opportunities with them in Chicago, where she became a manicurist at a barbershop. After serving in France in World War I, her brothers were impressed by the French attitude toward African Americans and women. In France women could be pilots. Bessie decided to make that true in the United States, but no white aviators would teach her. Bessie became fluent in French. Backed by the *Chicago Defender*, a black newspaper that helped her raise funds, she went to France. She made newspaper headlines in 1921, when she returned to America as a licensed pilot. Closed out of aviation jobs, she began flying open planes in air shows, doing barrel rolls, loop-the-loops, and parachute jumps to earn money for her "dream school." Bessie hoped to "uplift the Negro race" by helping others become pilots. She returned to the skies even after an accident landed her in the hospital for three months. Then, as her dream grew closer, the secondhand plane she had just bought suddenly tumbled into a tailspin, flipping her out. Over ten thousand people filed past her coffin, but memories of brave Bessie faded in the bright light of a more glamorous aviator. (See also Amelia Earhart.)

Michael Collins (1930–)

Michael Collins may be remembered as the Apollo 11 astronaut who got the much less glamorous—but absolutely necessary— job of staying in the command module spacecraft, while Neil Armstrong and Buzz Aldrin cavorted on the moon to gather rocks, set up experiments, and plant the American flag. Certainly, Michael Collins was as well qualified. A graduate of West Point, he had an Air Force commission and attended the Aerospace Research Pilot School. He was so dedicated to flight that he chose to have very complicated spinal surgery when that was his only chance of being able to continue flying. Fortunately, it was successful. Collins became the director of the National Air and Space Museum from 1971 to 1978. Each day he walked beneath the craft he had piloted to the moon. (See also Neil Armstrong and Edwin "Buzz" Aldrin, Jr.)

Christopher Columbus (1451–1506)

By the time the navigator from Genoa was pitching his plan for reaching the Indies to the kings of Portugal and England, he had already visited Iceland and sailed down the African coast. Columbus was convinced that the best way to reach the fabled riches of the East was to sail west. In Spain most of the experts advised against him, but Columbus persisted. On August 3, 1492, with a copy of *The Travels of Marco Polo* and a letter of introduction to the descendant of Kublai Khan, he set off for the Indies with three ships and ninety men. Ten weeks later he landed . . . on an island in the Bahamas. Certain that he was near the coast of Asia, he sailed around the area in search of Japan. Instead, he reached Cuba and later Hispaniola, where he left some of his crew. His next expedition with seventeen ships returned to Hispaniola to establish a settlement. Columbus, like the most advanced mapmakers of his day, thought that the world was much smaller than it is. He remained convinced that he had reached the East Indies until his death. As much later research suggests, some of the people he encountered may have been descendants of the Chinese sailors in Zheng He's fleet, who were swept ashore in a tropical storm. (See also Zheng He.)

James Cook (1728–1779)

The son of a Scottish farm worker, Cook probably added more to our information about the world than any single explorer. He distinguished himself as a meticulous marine surveyor in North America, charting the St. Lawrence River and the coast of Newfoundland. Once about every hundred years Venus crosses over the sun. Actually, two transits of Venus occur: the second eight years after the first. The event gave the British a good excuse to observe the transit in Tahiti, and then to search for

Terra Australis Incognita, the huge unknown southern continent that geographers imagined was a counterbalance to the land masses of the north. Britain wanted to claim the new continent before France! After completing the astronomical work in Tahiti, Cook crisscrossed the south Pacific to chart New Zealand and discover Australia. The Royal Geographical Society gave him a medal, but made much more fuss about one of their own, Joseph Banks, who had funded "scientifics." On Cook's next voyage, he was the first to cross the Antarctic Circle, coming within 1,250 miles of the South Pole and proving Terra Australis Incognita did not exist. His brilliant career ended in the Sandwich Islands, which we know by their original name, Hawaii. At first, Cook was welcomed as a reincarnation of Lono, the god of harvests. An unusually kind and generous man, Cook was respectful of other cultures. While he was trying to settle an argument onshore, his ship fired cannons without such an order from Cook himself. Frightened, the natives killed him.

Hernando Cortés (1485–1547)

When Cortés first arrived in Tenochtitlan, the Aztec capital, he pretended to be the great plumed-serpent god, Quetzalcoatl, returning from a visit with the Sun god. Cortés soon took Montezuma hostage as a "guest" and forced him to swear loyalty to the King of Spain. A collection of treasures began. Meanwhile, Cortés was in a power struggle to keep his command in Mexico. He left Pedro de Alvarado in charge while he went to Veracruz to stop the attempt. When Cortés returned, Tenochtitlan was at war. Alvarado's soldiers had killed huge numbers of Aztecs who were having a religious festival. The

Spaniards had guns, but the Aztecs were far greater in number. Montezuma tried to persuade his subjects to make peace with the Spaniards. The Aztecs were so angry that they stoned him to death. Cortés and Alvarado managed to escape the mob, but many Spaniards were killed. Two years later Cortés returned. Tenochtitlan was a breathtaking city, built on an island in the middle of a lake. After a siege of eighty days, it fell to the Spaniards. Mexico City is built on the site and some of the magnificent pyramids still remain.

Vasco da Gama (1460–1524)

Muslim merchant ships had been traveling between Africa and rich cities across the Indian Ocean for years. Vasco da Gama, the son of a Portuguese governor and a Knight Commander of the Military Order of Christ, was the first European to make a sea voyage to India. What a welcome he received when he returned to Portugal in 1499 with samples of spices! Two ships had been sacrificed after half the crew had died from scurvy, but Portugal now had a direct source for spices. King Manuel assumed a grandiose title: "Lord of the conquest, navigation, and commerce of Ethiopia, Arabia, Persia, and India." When a later expedition under Pedro Alvares Cabral arrived in Calicut, Arab traders attacked the "infidels." In response, Cabral's cannons attacked the innocent East Indians. In 1502 da Gama sailed toward Calicut. His warships stopped a Muslim ship at sea packed with families returning from a pilgrimage to Mecca. After taking off any precious cargo but leaving the passengers on board, da Gama had the ship set on fire. The Portuguese bombarded and looted Calicut and other ports before establishing a permanent colony in India.

Charles Darwin (1809—1882)

In 1831 the British Admiralty gave Captain Robert Fitzroy a twofold mission: to chart the coast of South America and to fix the longitudes of many nations in the southern hemisphere. To these Fitzroy added a third: to prove that the details of creation in Genesis were scientifically correct. While Fitzroy's ship, HMS *Beagle,* was being rebuilt for the voyage, Darwin was completing his studies for the ministry at Cambridge. He shared his passion for natural history with another clergyman, Professor Henslow, a botany professor. "Botanizing" and "geologizing" were seen as suitable hobbies for vicars, rather than as serious sciences. Young Darwin hoped to support Fitzroy's views about Genesis. During the voyage, which lasted almost five years (1831–1836), Darwin spent as much time on land as possible, making detailed observations of all he saw, but what he saw made him question the Biblical account of creation. He collected thousands of specimens, which he carefully packed and shipped off to Henslow. Upon his return he spent three years classifying his specimens and preparing the *Journal of Researches into the Geology and Natural History of the Various Countries visited by H.M.S.* Beagle. It was not until 1859, however, that he published his most controversial work, *On the Origins of Species.*

Samuel de Champlain (1567–1635)

French fur traders already had established a trading post with the native Montagnais people, when Samuel de Champlain, a navigator and geographer, sailed up the St. Lawrence River to the falls at Montreal in 1604. Champlain drew amazingly accurate maps based on what the Montagnais people told him. The maps included Hudson Bay and the Great Lakes, which Champlain would explore himself in the coming years. The lakes were so large that he thought they surely must connect with the Pacific Ocean. He went to France, and returned the next year with a group of settlers to Acadia on the Bay of Fundy. Many settlers died of scurvy, but more arrived. Champlain continued searching for a better site. He mapped the Atlantic coastline as far south as Masschusetts. In 1608 he founded the trading post that would become the city of Quebec. In 1612, with the title of Lieutenant to the Viceroy of New France, he had three goals: to explore the continent, to find a water route to the Pacific, and to convert the natives to Christianity. He won the allegiance of the Hurons, Algonquins, and Montagnais by joining with them against their enemy, the Iroquois. The Hurons cared for Champlain when he was wounded in a battle. While recovering, Champlain wrote a detailed account of Huron customs. He returned to France repeatedly to drum up support for New France: settlers, missionaries, supplies, and money. All were needed to keep Quebec going and allow Champlain to explore the West.

Catalina de Erauso (1585–1650?)

In seventeenth-century Spain, if a woman wore men's clothing or a man wore women's clothing, the punishment was death. But how else could Catalina de Erauso avoid becoming a nun? Stealing a needle, thread, and scissors, she slipped out of the convent at night. She remodeled her long skirt into pants and cut her hair. First she found work as a stable hand and then as a cabin boy. Sailing to South America, she was still fearful of being discovered. She joined the Spanish army and spent the next thirteen years on a remote outpost in Peru as a soldier. Next she tried mining, first in Chile and then in Argentina. Along with a ragtag group of companions, she crossed the uncharted Andes. Lost in the bitter cold, all but Catalina froze to death. She rejoined the army. During a street fight in a small town, she slipped into a church for cover, but put herself in danger by confessing to the priest. Instead of jail and death, she was given an army pension. Yet back in Spain, she could not fit in. She left for Rome, but en route, she was first jailed as a spy in France and then robbed and harassed on her release. Finally reaching Rome, she had an audience with the Pope. Her strange past made it hard for her to find comfort in Europe—or any-where. She returned to South America. No longer able to serve as a soldier, she became a mule caravan driver.

Sir Francis Drake (1540–1596)

Starting life in abject poverty, Drake was apprenticed to a captain of a coastal freighter when he was about twelve years old. He continued sailing toward wealth and position, honing his navigational skills on slave ships along the African coast and then in the New World. He smuggled goods to Spanish colonists, who were eager to avoid the mother country's heavy taxes, and pirated Spanish and Portuguese ships. He began to waylay the mule trains carrying gold and silver from South American mines to ports for shipment to Spain, and pillaged Cartagena and other towns. By 1573 he was a very rich man with a powerful friend, the Queen of England. In response to Queen Elizabeth's unwillingness to stop Drake, indeed her encouragement of him, in 1588 King Philip II sent the mighty Spanish Armada to punish England. Vice-Admiral Drake played a leading role in helping England destroy the Spanish fleet and become the world's leading naval power. As a further insult, Drake burned Sagres, the site of Prince Henry the Navigator's home. Drake died of a fever in the Caribbean. Until as recently as 2003, a complex hoax perpetuated the idea that Drake landed in California near San Francisco in 1579, while circumnavigating the world.

Jean Baptiste Pointe du Sable (1745–1818)

Born in Haiti, the son of an African-born slave and a French mariner, du Sable was educated in France. At age seventeen, he was on his way to New Orleans when his ship was wrecked. Hearing that the city was under Spanish control, he made his way up the Mississippi and then northeast along the Illinois River. About that time, the Treaty of Paris (1762) ended the French and Indian War, and France ceded its claims to the lands east of the Mississippi to England. Du Sable married a

Potawatomi woman. Her name, Catherine, suggests she had a French father. In 1772 du Sable started a trading post, Eschikagou, at the mouth of the Chicago River. In a few years, du Sable added barns and a comfortable home to his original building. Eschikagou was a perfect business location: fur trappers and lumbermen from Canada, as well as from the British colonies, made it so successful that it became a permanent settlement. In 1796 the first births were recorded in what was by then called Chicago.

Amelia Earhart (1897–1937)

Her first plane ride convinced Amelia she had to learn how to fly. A middle-class girl who grew up in Kansas, she took a job at the phone company to pay for flying lessons and bought her first plane within the same year. With elegant blond good looks, Amelia quickly became a celebrity, setting one record after another: the first woman passenger to cross the Atlantic, the first woman to fly coast to coast, the first woman pilot to cross the Atlantic, and more. Unlike Bessie Coleman, she had access to the best planes available. George Putnam, the publisher of Amelia's books and her husband, encouraged each new, and more dangerous, record-breaking flight. In 1937, with the world rooting for her, Amelia and her navigator, Fred Noonan, set off to circle the globe. Her plane was last seen taking off from New Guinea on June 29, 1937. Myth and mystery have surrounded Amelia Earhart ever since. (See also Bessie Coleman.)

Sylvia Earle (1935–)

When she learned to scuba dive as a teen, Sylvia Earle found her life's work! In 1970 she led a group of women scientists on an experiment of interest to NASA: what happens when people live in isolation for a prolonged period? But instead of outer space, Sylvia Earle and the "aquababes," as they were dubbed, did their work underwater. The media attention the project attracted was a chance to speak out for the need to protect the oceans and their riches. To increase awareness of ocean life, Sylvia collaborated on a film about migrating humpback whales. Earle's further explorations focused on the deep ocean, where she discovered amazing new worlds of plants and animals. She cofounded Deep Ocean Engineering and Deep Ocean Technologies with her husband to create submersibles that let scientists study the sea at previously unreachable depths. She served as chief scientist for the National Oceanic and Atmospheric Association and as Honorary President of the Explorers Club. Her books make the complexities of oceanography and marine biology understandable to nonscientists. Perhaps Sylvia is doing most for the planet as the National Geographic Society's explorer-in-residence, where she educates millions of adults and kids through the National Geographic website and publications.

Egeria (300s)

In 330 CE, with Rome besieged by waves of invaders, Emperor Constantine made the ancient city of Byzantium the capital of the Roman Empire. He renamed it Constantinople. During the reign of a later Byzantine emperor, Theodosius the Great, a remarkable nun, Egeria, made a *perigrinata,* or pilgrimage, to

Constantinople and other Near Eastern countries. She was exploring the sites of Biblical references such as Mount Sinai and the tombs of Job and St. Thomas the Apostle. Egeria may have been related to the emperor, who also came from Galicia in Spain. Clearly she was important: military escorts, bishops, and high-ranking clergy accompanied her. Egeria kept a diary in the form of letters, as if to share her experiences. In 1884, a fragment of it was discovered in the library of a monastery in Arezzo, Italy.

Margaret Fontaine (1862–1939)

In 1940 a fabulous bequest, over 22,000 butterflies, arrived at the Norwich Castle Museum in England from Margaret Fontaine. The Fontaine-Neilly Collection had been carefully labeled and organized in the drawers of ten display cases. Along with the gift was a padlocked lacquered box, which was not to be opened until April 15, 1978. The box held Margaret's "diaries," which she had started on April 15, 1898, when she was not quite sixteen. Each April 15 for more than sixty years, Margaret had carefully entered notes made during the previous year in a ledger book. Along with photos, picture postcards, and her own drawings, the ledgers follow her explorations of much of the world with a very particular bias: that of a very romantic lepidopterist or butterfly expert. One of eight children in the poor branch of an upper-class family, Margaret was introduced to the Victorian craze of "netting" by one uncle. Thanks to another uncle, she had a modest yearly income, which enabled her to travel. The pursuit of butterflies became a passion. Traveling with a sister or cousin, she visited Belgium, Switzerland,

France, Italy, and Spain. Increasingly, Margaret struck out on her own: Sicily, Corsica, Hungary, Austria, Greece, the Middle East, Turkey, Africa, India, Tibet, New Guinea, Fiji, Australia, the United States, and much of South America. She became a respected collector. It was in Syria that she met Khalil Neilly, who so convinced her of his love that she married him. Although Khalil was fifteen years younger and "of a class far beneath" hers, they were happy. There were always more butterflies to be found! Finally, at age 77, Margaret collapsed on a roadside in Trinidad. Her net was nearby.

Sir John Franklin (1786–1847)

Admiral John Barrow wanted to claim any still-uncharted lands for England. Since England no longer needed such a large navy, many brave officers became available for his projects. Sir John Franklin was one of them. When the British government announced a prize for discovering the Northwest Passage as an antidote to the Russian presence in the area, Barrow was obsessed. Sir John, who became known as "the man who ate his boots" when food supplies ran out on an earlier voyage, was willing to lead repeated unsuccessful attempts to find the Northwest Passage. When his last expedition disappeared in 1845, "Barrow's Boys" spent years looking for him, adding immensely to knowledge of the Arctic in the process. In 1854 a Hudson Bay Company official recovered silverware with Franklin's initials and discouraging clues from the natives. A record left on King William Island established that Sir John had died on June 11, 1847. (See also Sir John Ross.)

Yuri Gagarin (1934–1968)

On October 4, 1957, the Soviets amazed the world with Sputnik, the first satellite to circle the earth. A month later they launched a much heavier satellite, weighing over a thousand pounds. It carried a dog whose life signs were monitored and sent to earth. The fact that the United States was caught "sleeping under a Soviet moon," to paraphrase Nikita Khrushchev, helped Senator John F. Kennedy become President Kennedy in 1960. Even though the United States increased its efforts, the Soviets continued to lead the "space war." Soviet cosmonauts were younger than their American counterparts, most of whom had seen combat and were very experienced test pilots and engineers. Yuri Gagarin had grown up on a collective farm and joined the Soviet Air Force in 1955. Only twenty-seven years old, he became the first man in space and almost completed an orbit of the Earth, staying aloft for well over an hour. His spaceship *Vostok* traveled east over Japan, and Gagarin parachuted to safety over Turkey as planned. Dazzled by what he saw, he said, "People of the world, let us safeguard and enhance this beauty—not destroy it." He died a few years later while testing an airplane.

Genghis Khan (1162–1227)

Genghis Khan means "Master of All between the Oceans." In the first quarter of the thirteenth century, this son of a nomad united the nomadic tribes of Mongolia, codifying laws and organizing a fiercely efficient army that crossed the Gobi Desert and conquered China. Expert horsemen and archers, the

Mongols swept down from the north, conquering lands from Russia to Syria, from Hungary to Korea. Following the death of Genghis Khan, his sons carried on his drive into Asia Minor and Europe, creating a vast empire. His grandson was Kublai Khan, the great Khan, whom Marco Polo served.

John Glenn (1921–)

When World War II started, John left college to attend Naval Aviation School. In 1942 he was commissioned in the Marine Corps. Soon he was flying fighter planes in the Pacific, where his daring and bravery were apparent. After the war ended, America was trying to broker a peace agreement in China between the Nationalist government and Communist insurgents. Captain Glenn, still a marine, was the operations officer for a squadron of American pilots known as the North China Patrol. After various assignments, he was piloting Sabre fighter planes in the Korean War. Next Glenn became a test pilot and set a speed record: 3 hours 23 minutes between New York and Los Angeles. In 1959 NASA selected him to be one of seven Project Mercury Astronauts. In 1962 John Glenn became the first American to orbit the earth! The country was ecstatic. His success gave momentum to the dream of reaching the moon. After retiring from NASA and working for business, Colonel Glenn became Senator Glenn (1974–1999). Before leaving office, he visited outer space once again on the space shuttle *Discovery*. One assignment was to deliver the platform for the Hubble telescope; among its other missions were studies of microgravity and the aging process.

Mary Hall (1857–1912)

Mary Hall took a year to prepare to go from Cape Town to Cairo by traveling around South Africa. Unlike most Europeans, she felt safer with the natives without a gun and by herself. She teasingly said she counted on her terrier, Mafeking, to warn her of any threats from wild animals. Staying at missions or in native villages, Miss Hall traveled seven thousand miles in seven months: She sailed up the Shire River to Port Herald, took a train to Lake Nyasa, crossing Lake Tanganyika by steamer and mission dugout canoe. From there she trekked on to Lake Victoria and detoured east to Nairobi by rail and rickshaw. Reaching Lake Albert and Lake Gondokoro, she took the relatively common route down the Nile to Khartoum and Cairo. Native Africans honored her as a queen, yet this brave woman is overlooked in books about travelers and explorers. Copies of her book, *A Woman's Trek from Cape Town to Cairo,* are hard to find. Perhaps she was considered too outrageous for her time.

Heather Halstead (1974–)

Heather Halstead created a new kind of exploration for the twenty-first century. Soon after her graduation from Dartmouth College with a major in social history and education, she inherited some money. She used it to become the creator and cocaptain of a two-year expedition around the world on the *Makulu II,* a sailboat. What made this expedition unique was the ship's interactive website, linking it to a network of underserved classrooms. Students and their teachers were able to follow the boat's voyage and use it as a springboard for learning geography, natural sciences, math, and ocean systems, as well as different cultures. The voyages continue as enthusiastic young educators, much like Peace Corps workers, crew the ship, posing problems and responding to requests from an expanding number of students. Heather herself works at planning the focus of the trips and finding funding for them. Anyone can visit the *Makulu II* at www.reachtheworld.org.

Hanno of Carthage (680 BC–530 BC)

Carthage was an important Phoenician colony that became an imperial power. The very first "log of discovery" and the first known description of Africa, complete with an erupting volcano, was inscribed in a Carthaginian temple. It tells how Hanno of Carthage sailed along the coast of West Africa with a fleet of sixty ships. Each ship held fifty oarsmen and was packed with settlers and supplies. The travelers saw elephants and hippos; they met hostile and friendly natives. After leaving settlers at Arambys, the last of several sites, Hanno continued south, exploring the coast as far as the modern state of Gabon. That's most probably where he saw the "little hairy people," which he later learned were called gorillas. It's generally believed that a temple priest interviewed sailors, not Hanno himself. Scholars have been guessing at modern equivalents of the places the temple inscription mentions.

Queen Hatshepsut (1501–1468 BC)

While statues of Queen Hatshepsut show her wearing the male nemes (headdress), shendy (kilt), and false beard, she made no attempt to conceal her sex in other representations or writings. As an Egyptian woman, she had many more rights than women in other parts of the world were to have for centuries. And she used them. The charismatic queen sent five ships with thirty rowers each to the Land of Punt, which now is probably Somalia. The paintings at Deir al-Bahri so accurately detail the trip that it's possible to identify which species of fish are shown. In addition to myrrh for the temple gardens, the ships brought back ivory, ebony, and frankincense. When Hatshepsut's nephew, the child of her half-brother husband and a concubine, became Tutmose III, he had her name hacked off buildings and statues; he had the temple battered down. Years later, archaeologists uncovered it. Although the queen had the slaves who built her tomb killed to protect the secret of its hiding place, the tomb was soon pillaged. Even her mummy and the case with her heart was destroyed—quite possibly at her nephew's orders.

Zheng He (1371–1435)

The third Emperor of the Ming Dynasty put his talented slave, Zheng He, in charge of China's navy. In a short period (1425–1433) Zheng He assembled the largest fleet the world would see until the twentieth century! Its magnificent ships dwarfed those of Europe. Zheng He made major voyages, reaching not only many other countries of the Far East but India, Africa, and even, quite possibly, America—seventy years before Columbus! Scientists and astrologers came along to study and collect plants and animals and to observe the stars. Among the most amazing animals brought back to China were the giraffe, the celestial horse (the zebra), the celestial stag (the oryx), and camel-birds (ostriches). The next Ming emperor, however, destroyed the navy. Ships with more than three masts were forbidden. Logs of Zheng He's voyages and even the observations of the naturalists were suppressed. The discovery of a stone pillar in a Fujian province in the 1930s greatly helped scholars confirm this glorious period of the Middle Kingdom.

Henry the Navigator (1394–1460)

When the Roman Empire finally collapsed, the Catholic Church became the main unifying power in Europe. The Church's view of the world, based on a narrow reading of the Bible, stifled the progress of science and geography. Meanwhile, the Islamic Empire kept expanding its mastery of the seas and of trade. As the Middle Ages ended, a new spirit was growing, a kind of rebirth called the Renaissance. With the rediscovery of classical texts and aesthetics, art and science flourished. In Portugal, then the smallest country in Europe, King John's third son, Henry, a man who hardly ever voyaged far from his castle in Sagres on the southwest coast, directed all his energies and wealth to exploration. His work prepared little Portugal for a leading role in the Age of Discovery, which was just beginning at the time of Henry's death.

Matthew Henson (1866–1955)

Living in Washington, D.C., with a cruel uncle, Matthew ran away when his father died. At age thirteen, he started going to sea, gaining skills with every voyage. Between trips, he clerked at Steinmetz's marine supply store in Washington, D.C. Steinmetz enthusiastically recommended his young clerk to Robert Peary, who was going to chart the jungles of Nicaragua for the United States government. Henson's map-making skills were invaluable. Peary asked him to collaborate with him on reaching the North Pole. They made several trips to the Arctic. Henson quickly learned to speak Inuit and how to build sledges and handle dog teams. In 1909, after days of forced marches, they reached the pole. Henson marked it with a flag made from Mrs. Peary's black taffeta petticoat. On their return to the United States, they found that Dr. Frederick Cook claimed he had reached the pole a year earlier. In the ensuing dispute, Peary took all the credit for himself! He did nothing to help Henson advance beyond the limits that were open to most African Americans at the time. Fortunately, Admiral Donald B. MacMillan championed his cause; Henson was made a life member of the Explorers Club in 1947. Thanks to the club's efforts, Henson finally received just recognition. The year before his death, President Eisenhower presented him with the Congressional Medal. His family expressed their gratitude by donating half of Matthew's life insurance money to the Explorers Club. In 1966 the United States Post Office issued a stamp showing Henson and Peary together. (See also Robert Peary.)

Edmund Hillary (1919–)

At 29,028 feet, Mt. Everest is the world's highest mountain peak. Just before the coronation of Queen Elizabeth II, Edmund Hillary of New Zealand and Tenzing Norgay of Nepal became the first to reach the mountain's summit. With neither oxygen nor high-tech gear, they proved that the climb was possible. Britain knighted Hillary and gave Norgay the George Medal. Hillary started mountaineering as a teenager, climbing mountains in New Zealand. Although he made his living as a beekeeper, he managed to climb mountains in the Alps and had reached eleven peaks of over 20,000 feet in the Himalayas before tackling Everest. During the fifty-plus years following their triumph, others continue to challenge Everest. It remains extremely dangerous, even though it's been "tamed," to use Sir Edmund's term, with countless aluminum ladders and miles of fixed rope. Sir Edmund participated in other expeditions, most notably crossing Antarctica and following the Ganges River to its source. He has devoted much of his life to helping Nepal to build schools, clinics, and hospitals. As Nepal's trees were being cut down to provide fuel for climbing expeditions, he guided the establishment of the Mt. Everest National Forest with aid from New Zealand. (See also Tenzing Norgay.)

Henry Hudson (?–1611)

The most skilled navigator of his age, Hudson made four voyages to find a northern passage to the Orient. The British Muscovy company funded the first two unsuccessful expeditions in 1607 and 1608. In 1609, the Dutch East India Company gave him the same commission. Before sailing, Hudson had heard of an alternate route to the East through north-west straits. So when his ship, the *Half Moon,* ran into arctic ice, he sailed across the Atlantic, down the eastern coast of North America, and into New York harbor. He continued up what became the Hudson River as far as what is now Albany. While the river did not lead to China, the Dutch happily claimed it. Within a year their fur traders were active. Furious, England placed tight restrictions on Hudson. A British merchant group gave him another commission to find an Arctic passage. On April 17, 1610, Hudson and a crew of twenty-two men sailed north in the *Discovery.* Under terrible pressure, Hudson seemed to make bad judgments, which alienated the crew, according to the expedition's four survivors. They were tried for mutiny but eventually set free.

Mae Jemison, MD (1956–)

The first African-American woman in space combines unusual skills and achievements with deep social commitment. In addition to being an astronaut, she's a physician, research scientist, photographer, educator, graphic artist, and a speaker of Japanese, Russian, and Swahili. And more. Born in Alabama, Dr. Jemison grew up in Chicago. After attending public schools, she entered Stanford at just sixteen. Graduating not only with a degree in chemical engineering, she also completed requirements for a degree in African and African-American studies. After medical school at Cornell University, Dr. Jemison worked in Africa as a doctor and in a refugee camp in Thailand. As an astronaut, she became the science specialist on an eight-day U.S. Spacelab mission with Japan that completed forty-four experiments. After leaving NASA in 1993, she founded the Jemison Group in Houston, Texas, to implement advanced health care technologies suited to individuals from nonindustrial cultures. Invited to teach a course at Dartmouth College, she continues on the faculty as director of the Institute for Advancing Technology in Developing Countries. She also chairs "The Earth We Share," a camp where high school–age students from all over the world gather to ponder global problems.

Mary Kingsley (1863–1900)

Had she been given every opportunity, Kingsley's accomplishments would be amazing. On her two extended trips to West Africa in 1893 and 1895, she became the first European to make an overland crossing between the Ogooue and the Remboue Rivers and the first woman to summit Mt. Cameroon. Even now, her studies of the Fang people remain outstanding. Her letters, speeches, and books sparkle with good humor. However, Mary spent her first thirty years shut in a dark, dreary house. When she was ten, her uneducated mother went to bed and stayed there. Mary became her nurse and ran the household. Her father was often away, serving as personal physician to wealthy travelers. He totally opposed education for girls. How did she learn to read? Perhaps her younger brother, Charles, had a primer. Her father's library was full of books about exploration. Mary found heroes who were models of bravery, perseverance, and duty. And it was duty that made

Mary care for her parents until they both died and she was finally free to fulfill her dreams. Within months she was on her way to West Africa. In addition to her other plans, she was to collect fish specimens for the British Museum. Africans taught her how to fish using nets of pineapple plant fibers. Returning to England to help her brother, she wrote the first of her two books and also raised money for her second trip by giving lectures. Her outspoken respect for African cultures upset the clergy. After her second trip and second book, though, Mary was a celebrity. The government minister for Africa secretly met with her for advice, yet she'd put aside her own life to nurse a friend or relative. And finally, duty caused Mary's early death. During the Boer War in South Africa, she nursed prisoners and caught typhoid from them. Mary was buried at sea, off the Cape of Good Hope, below the continent she considered home.

Meriwether Lewis (1774–1809)

The Louisiana Purchase gave President Thomas Jefferson the chance to fulfill his long-held dream: to explore the West and find a waterway to the Pacific. He chose his personal secretary, Meriwether Lewis, "of undaunted courage," to lead the expedition. Farmer, soldier, student of botany, astronomy, and medicine, Lewis combined an infectious curiosity with excellent wilderness skills. His leadership skills won him the unquestioned loyalty of the Corps of Discovery, the carefully chosen group of some thirty men, plus a young Shoshone woman, Sacagawea. The goals of the trip included observations of plants and animals, fixing the latitude and longitude of the Mississippi and Missouri

Rivers by celestial navigation, as well as interactions with many groups of Indians. Jefferson wanted to convince them that they had a beneficent and powerful new "father" in Washington. Jefferson believed that the fur trade would be all the more profitable through strong partnerships with the Indians. Lewis and his cocaptain, William Clark, kept journals of the expedition's activities as well as detailed observations of nature and tribal peoples. On their triumphant return to the United States, Lewis sought expert help from botanists, naturalists, and astronomers in preparing the journals for publication. At the same time, however, President Jefferson also appointed him governor of the Louisiana Territory, a political minefield where Lewis made enemies. Disappointed by the young woman he hoped to marry and plagued by recurring bouts of malaria, which he treated with opium and whiskey, Lewis seemed unable to carry out his overwhelming duties. The depression that had also affected his father, and which Lewis had struggled with earlier, overcame him. He committed suicide. (See also William Clark, Sacagawea, and York.)

David Livingstone (1813–1873)

By the age of ten David Livingstone was working at a cotton mill near Glasgow, Scotland. In spite of terrible poverty, he learned enough math, Latin, and Greek to become a physician and then an ordained missionary. Hoping to stop the slave trade, he went to South Africa as a missionary. He learned to speak Setswana, and, unlike most Europeans, he treated the tribal people with respect. His idea of training Africans to be missionaries was rejected by the mission directors in London.

Within a few years, Livingstone was devoting himself to exploring the continent, surviving unimaginable hardships, including an attack by a lion. When he returned to England, he was a hero. A book describing his trek across the continent sold well. At last, he was able to provide his family with a comfortable life, but he soon left them to return to Africa. After the famous meeting with Stanley, Livingstone insisted on remaining in Africa, even though he clearly was not well. After his death, his two servants embalmed his body with salt and wrapped it in bark. Along with his journals and notes, they carried his body to Zanzibar, a trek of one thousand miles that took the better part of a year. His body was returned to England and is buried in Westminster Abbey. But first they had wrapped his heart and internal organs in calico and buried them in Africa. (See Henry M. Stanley.)

Ferdinand Magellan (1480–1521)

Still a child, Magellan was a page in the Portuguese court; as a young man, he became a squire, in charge of provisioning ships for explorers. Next, he served Portugal as a naval officer in Francisco de Almeida's twenty-one-ship fleet. (Under de Almeida, the Portuguese destroyed Mombasa and burned Indian cities in an attempt to seize control of trade from the Arabs.) Wounded in battle in the Indian Ocean and then falsely accused of corruption, Magellan lost the confidence of King Manuel. With permission to serve elsewhere, Magellan and his friend, Ruy Faleiro, a geographer/astronomer, went to Spain, where they were made honorary nobles. In 1494, with the help of the Pope, Spain and Portugal agreed to divide the world for purposes of exploration. But where were the dividing lines in the east? Magellan proposed to sail west to the Spice Islands (the Moluccas) to prove they were on the Spanish side. And . . . to circle the world in the process! Probably through Faleiro, Magellan knew of a possible water passage across South America located somewhere below Brazil. The young king of Spain quickly provided Magellan with a small fleet, in spite of his advisers, who opposed an expedition led by a foreigner.

Maria Sibylla Merian (1647–1717)

Maria Sibylla Merian came from a family of Frankfurt artists. Her early engravings of flowers were published as embroidery patterns. Next came a book of European butterflies. When her marriage failed, she joined a Protestant spiritual community based at a castle in the Netherlands. The owner of the castle had collections of natural objects from the Dutch colonies: dried flowers, butterflies, and moths. They were larger and more brilliantly colored than any she had seen in Europe. Maria yearned to observe them in nature. Somehow she had to get to Suriname. Finally, the Dutch government gave her a stipend. At age fifty-two, off she sailed to Suriname with her younger daughter. As word of the strange European woman spread, natives and former slaves living in the swamps and jungles of the interior brought her plants and insects—moths, butterflies, and spiders—in their pupa stage. She was the first observer anywhere to show their full life cycle and their host plants. When she returned to Europe her spectacular work was a great success. Peter the Great and other royals had to add it to their collections.

Fridtjof Nansen (1861–1930)

Althought Nansen was an academic, a scientist, a statesman, and humanitarian who won the Nobel Peace Prize in 1922, he's best remembered as an arctic explorer. His squat boat, the *Fram,* was designed with just enough flexibility to respond to the pack ice without being crushed by it. Nansen's expedition left Norway in 1893. When the *Fram* was gripped in the ice, the drift to the west began, but the drift north was much less than expected. Finally, Nansen began to think that unless he reached the pole on foot, he would not reach it at all. Leaving his crew on the *Fram,* he set off north with Frederic Johansen. However, they had to turn back. Fortunately, they met Frederick Jackson, a British explorer and naturalist, who was spending five years on Franz Josef Land. A wealthy Englishman was sponsoring Jackson to "geologize," "botanize," and "naturalize" the area. Jackson had several assistants, who arrived and left by ship for much shorter periods. Jackson and Nansen sat up for forty hours, talking and talking. The British did all they could to make the Norwegians comfortable, from providing a hot bath—it was only possible for one person a day to have a bath—to hot food. The Norwegians returned home in 1896 on a British ship. The *Fram,* released from the ice north of Spitzbergen, sailed back to Norway in August of that same year.

Tenzing Norgay (1914–1986)

Born while his mother was on a Buddhist pilgrimage, Tenzing was given the name Norgay by a lama (a Buddhist monk).

Norgay means "fortunate." Tibet was closed to outsiders until 1945. Growing up in the shadow of Mt. Everest, young Tenzing felt pulled toward it. As a young teen, he left home for Darjeeling, India, where foreign expeditions originated. He worked as a porter and then as a guide. His skills were recognized. In 1952 a Swiss expedition invited him to join, not as a guide but as a climber. He came very close to the summit. The British Geological Society organized an expedition in 1953. Norgay and Edmund Hillary were the expedition's only climbers to reach the summit. For Norgay it was a spiritual experience as well as a physical achievement. Britain gave him its highest civilian reward, the George Medal. A celebrity, he was visited by the Prime Minister of India and other heads of state. Norgay headed the Institute of Mountaineering for over twenty years. Hillary remained his close friend until his death. In 2003, Norgay's son, Jamlin, and Hillary's grandson, Peter, returned to Mt. Everest to repeat their forbears' climb. (See also Edmund Hillary.)

Amos Nur (1938–)

Born in Israel, Dr. Nur earned a PhD in geophysics from Massachusetts Institute of Technology. He is the Wayne Loel Professor of Earth Sciences and a professor of geophysics at Stanford University. His specialty in geophysical exploration is wave propagation research: underwater tectonics. (See also Dr. Jean-Daniel Stanley.)

Mary Ann Parker (1755–1805?)

Captain John Parker (1749–1795) brought along his wife, Mary Ann, on the long and dangerous voyage to New South Wales (Australia). When he died of yellow fever two years after their return, she wrote and published the earliest known description of Australia by a traveler. Hoping to supplement her meager widow's mite, she dedicated the book "with permission" to the Princess of Wales. The book starts with a long list of subscribers, who must have paid the printing costs. Clearly an entertaining young woman, Mrs. Parker was fluent in several languages. She may have been invited to entertain the new Lieutenant Governor and his wife. The ship was carrying convicts, handpicked for their farming experience, and replacements to relieve the soldiers who had been in Australia for five years. On the return trip, the *Gorgon* salvaged the contents of a "storeship" that had been wrecked by an iceberg and brought to Cape Town, South Africa, by a skeleton crew. Mrs. Parker amusingly describes the ladies of the Cape, who were waited on hand and foot by servants. Like modern travel writers, she even has a few shopping suggestions.

Robert E. Peary (1856–1920)

A U.S. Navy officer with an engineering degree, Peary surveyed Nicaragua. It was being evaluated as a canal site, along with Panama. Matthew Henson, his helper on that expedition, became his partner for arctic exploration. Josephine, Peary's wife, came along on several arctic expeditions, and published *My Arctic Journal* in 1893. She wanted to prove that women could endure the extreme conditions explorers encounter.

Initially, Robert E. Peary established that Greenland was an island. The Eskimos had three enormous meteorites, which were especially prized because they contained iron. Peary said the Eskimos were "children and should be treated as such." He insisted on taking all three meteorites to the United States. The Inuit called Peary Piulerriaq, or "the Great Tormentor." Funded by a group of wealthy supporters, Peary had a well-equipped ship built to his specifications and named it the *Roosevelt*. With fur clothing made by Inuit women and dog teams expertly driven by Inuit men and Matthew Henson, Peary, whose toes suffered from frostbite, rode on a sledge as he directed an excruciatingly difficult—but successful—assault on the pole. He photographed Henson and the others beneath the flag that Henson had planted at the pole. (See also Matthew Henson.)

Annie Peck (1850–1935)

In 1895 Miss Annie Smith Peck was the third woman to climb the awesome Matterhorn in the Swiss-Italian Alps, but the first to do so wearing pants! She was also the first woman to attend the American School for Classical Studies in Athens. She taught Latin at Purdue University and Smith College, supplementing her modest salary with slide lectures of her climbing exploits. At fifty, she left teaching to devote her life to mountaineering. Her dream: to summit a "peak where no man had previously stood." Raising funds was a constant problem, and more than once the Swiss guides she hired lost their nerve. On her sixth attempt to reach the ice-capped summit of Mt. Huascaran in the Peruvian Andes, she succeeded! The Lima Geographic Society named the north peak of Mt. Huascaran Cumbre (peak) Ana Peck. Still able to move "like a squirrel" at age sixty-one, Miss Peck climbed the Coropuna in Peru, which was thought to be the highest mountain in South America. Competing against a team from Yale University, she reached the two highest peaks before the men had even reached the first. On each peak she planted a banner: VOTES FOR WOMEN.

Ida Pfeiffer (1797–1858)

After twenty-two years of marriage to Dr. Pfeiffer, her senior by some twenty-five years, and having raised sons who were almost adults, Ida Pfeiffer left Vienna in 1842. There was so much she wanted to see—and so little she missed. Undeterred by warnings of plague and "disturbances," Ida traveled around the Holy Land on horseback from Jerusalem to the Dead Sea. She went to Damascus, where she visited the Pasha's harem and joined a caravan for a two-week desert crossing. There were stops in Beirut, Cairo, and Italy. Her first book was published in German and quickly translated. It funded her next jaunt: Iceland via Scandinavia. *A Woman's Journey Round the World* documents a two and a half year voyage with some unusual side trips. For example, Ida spends an impromptu overnight with the Paras, an indigenous tribe, in the rain forest of Brazil, dining on monkey and parrot. Her sketchy account of her visit may be the first description of the Paras ever made. Her adventures became so well known that shipping companies and railroads began to beg Ida to take free passage. She went places Western women simply did not go. Each trip was more exotic, more dangerous.

Francisco Pizarro (1475–1541)

Two illiterate Spanish soldiers of fortune, Francisco Pizarro and his partner, Diego de Almagro, plundered the Inca empire. It stretched from beyond its northern capital, Quito, in present-day Ecuador, to below its southern capital, Cuzco, in what is now Peru. The Inca empire had about ten million people, who spoke more than twenty languages. You still can see their terraced fields engineered into steep, rocky hillsides and observe architectural and astronomical genius in the perfectly set, huge stones at Machu Picchu. But outside of the National Museum in Lima and a few churches, you'll see very little of the gold that fueled the brutal conquest.

Sailing from Panama, Pizarro crossed the Alps with horses and 180 men. After inviting the Emperor, Atahualpa, to visit his camp, Pizarro took him prisoner and had his large retinue slaughtered. To free Atahualpa, his subjects had to fill a seventeen-foot by twenty-two foot room with gold, piled as high as Atahualpa could reach. After the ransom was met, Pizarro had Atahualpa publicly strangled to death.

Marco Polo (1254–1324)

Traders from Europe bought the silks and spices of the East in Constantinople. In 1265, however, two Venetian brothers, Maffeo and Niccolo Polo, continued far beyond the city. Traveling overland, they reached the fabulous Mongol empire of Kublai Khan, who made the brothers his ambassadors. Open to ideas, the Khan sent them to ask the Pope for "a hundred learned men" and for holy oil from Jerusalem. They returned in 1275 with the oil but without the "learned men." Instead,

Niccolo offered the services of his son, Marco, a lad of seventeen. He became a loyal servant to Kublai Khan and traveled widely throughout his kingdom. When Marco finally returned to Venice, he was forty-one. Having crossed the mountains and deserts of Asia, as well as of India and Persia, he probably had seen more of the world than anyone in Europe. When his story was written by Rusticello of Pisa as *The Travels of Marco Polo* it was such a success that handwritten copies circulated throughout Europe. Most people thought that the book was a fantasy. In fact, calling something a "Marco Polo" meant it was unbelievable. Paper money! Who would use that?

John Wesley Powell (1834–1902)

When the Civil War started, Powell put aside his collections of rocks, mollusk shells, and pressed plants to serve the Union. A Confederate bullet hit his right arm and it had to be amputated. Powell returned to active service as soon as his wound had healed, although it continued to be painful. A major when he was discharged, Powell remained "the Major" to the students he taught, to the members of the expeditions he led, and to the Washington politicians he lobbied. He won the support of politicians for two of his projects: the United States Geological Survey, which mapped the entire country, and the Bureau of American Ethnology, which recorded Native American customs and life. Nobody, however, would listen to his environmentally advanced ideas about water use in the arid West. As an explorer, Powell organized an expedition to the Rocky Mountains in 1868. His wife, Emma, became the first woman to summit Pikes Peak, which was covered in thirty inches of snow that July. In 1869 and in 1871–73, Powell's expeditions were the first to explore fully the Colorado River and the Grand Canyon.

Alice Huyler Ramsey (1887–1983)

When Alice Huyler Ramsey asked her adoring husband for a horse, he surprised her with a bright red Maxwell touring car. He never could have imagined that almost fifty years later the American Automobile Association would honor her as its "Woman Motorist of the Century." In 1908 cars were still toys for the rich, and car dealers organized outings where owners drove a fixed course. When the Maxwell sales manager saw Alice drive, he had an idea. In 1903 Dr. H. Nelson Jackson had crossed the country in a one-cylinder Oldsmobile. In 1906 Ellis Whitman drove his Franklin from San Francisco to New York in thirty-three days. Two years later he cut the time to fifteen days. Now the Maxwell Company would sponsor the first woman to drive a car from New York to San Francisco: a pretty young mother, as well as a graduate of Vassar College. Alice's two sisters-in-law, Nettie and Maggie, and her friend, Hermione, came along for company, but Alice drove every mile of the way herself. And it was quite a trip! Road maps, as we know them, didn't exist, and paved roads were rare. Blowouts of the smooth canvas tires, broken axles, wheels that rolled off and disappeared, and the thirteen days it took to get across "the mud gumbo" of Iowa paled in comparison to inching across a gorge on a narrow Union Pacific track with just a single pair of rails.

Sally Ride (1951–)

Growing up in California, Sally Ride was an outstanding athlete as well as student. Graduating from Stanford with both a BS in physics and a BA in English, she went on to complete a PhD in physics there. NASA selected her as a candidate, and by 1979 she was eligible to be an orbit capsule communicator specialist. In June 1983 Sally Ride became the first American woman in space as a mission specialist aboard the *Challenger*. Space flight had become much more sophisticated in the twenty years since the Soviets had first put a woman in orbit. In addition to staying aloft, the five-person crew performed various scientific experiments and deployed a payload of satellites. She was training for a third mission in 1986 when the *Challenger* exploded shortly after liftoff. She left NASA in 1987. After directing the California Space Institute, she joined the University of California at San Diego as a physics professor. In 2001 Sally started Imaginary Lines, a program to support girls in pursuing science, and she also heads up EarthKAM, a NASA educational program for middle school students. In 2003, she joined the panel investigating the space shuttle *Columbia* disaster.

Sir James Clark Ross (1800–1862)

After starting his career at age eighteen as a junior officer in the Royal Navy under his uncle Commander John Ross, James sailed on expeditions to the Arctic under Edward Parry for ten years. When the elder Ross led a privately financed expedition to the high Arctic, James captained one of the ships. Trapped in pack ice for three years off of the Boothia Peninsula, the Rosses made extensive studies of the Polar Inuit and James became the first man to reach and identify the North Magnetic Pole (which has since shifted its position). In 1839 Captain Ross commanded the British expedition to reach the South Pole. At the same time, both the United States and France had sent expeditions with the same goal. However, neither of them was prepared for the Arctic. Ross's well-designed ships sailed farther south than those of anyone else for sixty years. He discovered a seemingly endless mass of floating ice between six hundred and one thousand feet thick, which is known as the Ross Ice Shelf. On his return, Queen Victoria knighted him. (See also Sir John Ross.)

Sir John Ross (1777–1856)

Royal Navy Commander John Ross and his nephew, James Clark Ross, were trying to find the Northwest Passage about the same time as Sir John Franklin. (In fact, Sir John Ross led one of the searches for Franklin.) England was also interested in creating a presence in the Arctic to counterbalance Russia's well-established claims. Sailing far north of the Arctic Circle, the Ross Expedition made a vivid impression on the natives. Polar Inuit had been cut off from Inuit groups to the south for so many years that they had begun to think that they were the only human beings in the world. They had even lost the knowledge of their traditional boats, the kayak and the larger umiak, as well as the bow and arrow. Fortunately, however, in 1860 Canadian Inuit traveling north reintroduced these lost traditions to their polar cousins. The poem "The Amazing Surprise" is based on an actual description of one of Ross's ships by an arctic Inuit, recorded by an anthropologist years later. Sir John was honored with gold medals by many geographical societies and was knighted in 1834. He also authored books describing his expeditions. (See also Sir James Clark Ross and Sir John Franklin.)

Sacagawea (1787?–1812)

As a young girl, Sacagawea was taken from her people, the Shoshone, in a raid by the Hidatsa. They gave her a Hidatsa name which links *sacaga* (bird) with *wea* (woman). According to Toussaint Charbonneau, a French Canadian fur trader who lived among the Hidatsa, he won Sacagawea and another Shoshone girl in a bet with Hidatsa warriors. When he was hired as a translator by Lewis and Clark, Charbonneau chose Sacagawea, then perhaps fifteen years old and six months pregnant, to accompany him. She spoke Hidatsa and Shoshone and would prove to be invaluable to the expedition. Meriwether Lewis attended her at the birth of a healthy boy, Jean-Baptiste, in February 1805, while the Corps of Discovery was wintering with the Mandans. The expedition was hoping to get horses from the Shoshone. Luckily, Sacagawea's brother had become the chief of the Shoshone!

Sacagawea was helpful in other ways: seeing a woman and child, Native Americans assumed the group was friendly. Sacagawea gathered wild vegetables, such as Jerusalem artichokes; berries; and herbs, such as licorice, which added nutrients and flavor to the meals. When the corps reached the Pacific and winter was about to set in, the captains decided to let everyone vote on where to make camp. Sacagawea and York were included. It was the first time that a Native American woman and an African American slave voted in North America. When the corps left the Northwest, Charbonneau was paid $500.33 for his services, his teepee, and his horse. Sacagawea received nothing at the time. Yet when Sacagawea died in 1812, William Clark adopted both Jean-Baptiste, whom he called Pomp, and his baby sister, Lisette. (See also William Clark, Meriwether Lewis, and York.)

Robert Falcon Scott (1868–1912)

In 1900 the Berlin Geographical Congress proclaimed an Antarctic Year, sparking expeditions from many countries, including Britain. Sir Clements Markham, "the father of British Antarctic exploration," promoted an English ethic: It is better to fail as amateurs than to succeed as professionals. Robert Falcon Scott of the Royal Navy, who commanded the first British expedition organized by the Royal Geographical Society, agreed. "To do without dogs," he wrote, "would make the conquest more nobly and splendidly won." Scott's bravery led to reckless decisions that compromised his own safety and that of his men. While his first expedition (1901–1903) provided useful information, his book *Voyage of the* Discovery made him a celebrity. When Captain Scott left for Antarctica in 1910, his ship carried three Caterpillar tractors, Siberian ponies, and a photographer to record his expected triumph. In Australia, however, Scott found a telegram from Roald Amundsen; he was also on his way to Antarctic waters. A race was on! Scott's ship, a bulky whaler, made slow progress. On land the tractors and ponies were useless. When Scott left base camp for a rush to the pole, he let an extra man come along at the last minute. Even though Scott's team now had dogs and skis, Scott abandoned them. Exhausted and disheartened, suffering with frostbite and scurvy, Scott and his crew froze to death on their return from the pole. Amundsen and his men returned safely. (See also Roald Amundsen and Ernest Shackleton.)

Ernest Shackleton (1874–1922)

When Ernest was sixteen, his father apprenticed him as a "boy" on a sailing ship for a shilling a month. By the time he was twenty-four, Shackleton was certified as a master in the Merchant Navy and a member of the Royal Geographical Society. He joined the National Antarctic Expedition led by Robert Falcon Scott of the Royal Navy. When Scott decided to make a madcap dash to the South Pole, he took Shackleton and just one other man. Shackleton became seriously ill. Scott, who had shot their dogs and refused to use his skis, blamed Shackleton for their failure to reach the pole. In 1909 Shackleton led his own expedition to the south and came within a hundred miles of the pole, beating Scott's record by 360 miles. Returning as a hero, Shackleton was knighted. Scott left on his last expedition to Antarctica in 1910, never to return. For his next try, Shackleton wanted to cross Antarctica from the Weddell Sea to the Ross Sea by way of the South Pole, which Amundsen had reached in 1912. Within weeks of sailing, the main ship, the *Endurance,* was caught and eventually crushed by pack ice. The men and dogs camped on the surrounding thick ice floe for months. They escaped this relative comfort in open boats, surviving incredible hardships. *South* is an amazing story of seamanship by a man whose first commitment was to the survival of his remarkable crew. (See also Roald Amundsen and Robert Falcon Scott.)

Richard Spruce (1817–1893)

A former teacher, Richard Spruce went to South America with two other self-taught naturalists, Henry Walter Bates and Alfred Russel Wallace. Once there, Spruce tended to work independently. He became the first botanist to collect plants along the Amazon, as well as the Orinoco and Negro river valleys. He divided areas into what we would now call ecological zones. Then he carefully collected all the plants of one zone before going on to the next. He made meticulously detailed drawings. Spruce was the first to study South American rubber plants. He also studied the cinchona tree, the source of quinine—which both prevented and cured malaria. By the time he returned to England in 1864, he had mapped rivers, recorded the vocabularies of over twenty native South American languages, and collected 30,000 plants. Unfortunately, his work never received proper recognition during his lifetime.

Sir Henry M. Stanley (1841–1904)

Sir Henry Morton Stanley started life in a British workhouse as John Rowlands. After sailing to New Orleans as a cabin boy, he was adopted by a merchant, who gave the young man his own name. During the Civil War, Stanley served in both the

Confederate Army and the Union Navy. He began working as a reporter for the *New York Herald*, which sent him to Africa to find Dr. Livingstone, the famous explorer who had mysteriously disappeared for two years while searching for the source of the Nile. Against all odds, Stanley found him. From then on their two names would be paired, yet they were very different men. Livingstone was an idealist who respected the Africans; Stanley was an opportunist who exploited them. Stanley returned to Africa in 1874 to lead an amazing boat trip the full length of the Lualaba and Congo Rivers that lasted 999 days. His book *In Darkest Africa* describes the trip. Then he convinced King Leopold of Belgium to establish a colony in the Congo, ironically called the Congo Free State. Stanley persuaded confused tribal leaders to sign away their lands to the king. The atrocities practiced were so brutal that the Belgium parliament finally took action to stop the king. Stanley later made speaking tours of the United States, England, and Australia. (See also David Livingstone.)

Jean-Daniel Stanley (1934-)

A senior scientist at the Smithsonian Institute of the Museum of Natural History in Washington, D.C., Dr. Stanley is a geological oceanographer. He's an expert on how rivers and oceans gradually change the globe by moving sediments to create underwater canyons and trenches. Using high-tech geophysical techniques such as slide-scan sonar for mapping, he has studied the Nile delta with a team of divers. Born in France, Dr. Stanley came to the United States as a young child and became an American citizen in 1946. Italy, Belgium, and France have honored him with gold medals for his work. (See also Amos Nur.)

Valentina Tereshkova (1937–)

Growing up during World War II, which claimed her father's life, Valentina started school at age eight and left when she was sixteen to work in a textile factory. She took correspondence courses to learn more about her work, but her hobby, parachuting, was more interesting. She was so skilled that she became the first person in the Soviet space program with no background as a test pilot, as well as the first woman in space. In 1963 Valentina orbited the earth forty-eight times and racked up more time in space in three days than all the American astronauts put together. After her flight, she went to a military air academy and graduated with honors. She was active in international women's organizations and was honored as a hero both by her own country and the United Nations. Premier Khruschev reportedly pushed her into marrying another cosmonaut, but they divorced. Little has been heard from Valentina since the breakup of the Soviet Union.

Charles Wyville Thomson (1830–1882)

Before the Challenger Expedition (1872–1876) it was commonly assumed that deep oceans were lifeless and that deep sea water was all the same temperature. Two academic biologists disagreed and proposed thoroughly surveying and mapping the world's oceans. Companies laying intercontinental cable lines across the ocean floors supported the idea. With Britain at the peak of its power, the Admiralty refitted a ship with laboratories and research equipment. Biologist Charles Wyville Thomson assembled an international team of six scientists, including the young Canadian, Sir John Murray, who would become famous. With a crew of 225 sailors, the work of the Challenger began in 1873 at the first of 362 workstations. Crisscrossing the oceans, the Challenger stopped at various ports of call, where scientists explored and made visual records of people and places. But the expedition's main work was at sea. The officers' journals complain of boredom with the repetitive surveying process: collecting, bottling, labeling. The tedious physical work, however, fell to the sailors. Over sixty of them deserted in ports. The huge amount of information collected was the basis for a new science: oceanography.

Vikings (750–1050)

The Vikings of Scandinavia—Sweden, Norway, and Denmark—were great boat builders. Their square-sailed merchant ships could hold up to twenty-five tons of cargo; their long, slender shallow troop ships, rowed by thirty to sixty oarsmen, could carry up to one hundred men and several horses. Oiled woolen sails rigged with horsehair added speed. So great was the Vikings' attachment to their boats that when they left this world to dwell with their god Odin in the great halls of Valhalla, they were often buried in boats with a battle-ax and other weapons. In Denmark their graves were marked with stones in the shape of ships. Long before Erik the Red and his son Leif Eriksson colonized Iceland and Greenland, Viking ships made forays to the British Isles and Ireland, where they founded Dublin. They turned to Europe, plundering Paris and sailing through the Strait of Gibraltar to attack North Africa. Vikings established colonies in the New World as early as 1000, but eventually abandoned them.

York (1770?–1831?)

William Clark's slave, the son of Old York and Rose, was born about the same time as Clark himself. When Clark's father died in 1799, he left William the family's slaves. Yet in his journal entries, Clark refers to York as "my servant." Knowing that the journals were to be the published record of the Lewis and Clark expedition, perhaps he did not wish to be remembered as a slave master. York worked hard and uncomplainingly during the expedition, enduring frostbite and extreme fatigue. The Indians were fascinated and delighted by him. He went about on his own with a gun, to hunt for game; when a vote was taken to determine a winter camp, York's vote was counted. Yet when the expedition returned to St. Louis in 1806, the other men were national heroes and well rewarded, but Clark refused to give York his freedom. He begged to be hired out so he could be near his family in Louisville, Kentucky. However, it suited Clark to keep York with him. He gave York two weeks to visit his family. When York seemed "sulky" on his return, Clark gave him a "severe trouncing" and threatened to hire him out to "a severe master," which he did. Although researchers question Clark's account, he claimed that he eventually freed York in either 1811 or 1816. Meanwhile, York's wife's owner had moved to

Tennessee. Apparently York never found his family. Years later, Clark told the author Washington Irving that York had died of cholera while on his way back to his master, supposedly "cursing freedom." (See also William Clark, Meriwether Lewis, and Sacagawea.)

Bibliography

Books

Adler, Marcus Nathan. *The Itinerary of Benjamin of Tudela: Critical Text, Translation, and Commentary.* London: first edition 1907.

Bond, Peter. *Zero G: Life and Survival in Space.* London, England: Cassell Illustrated Division, 1999.

Brown, Don. *Rare Treasures: Mary Anning and Her Remarkable Discoveries.* Boston, MA: Houghton Mifflin Company, 1999.
An accurate if sketchy telling of Mary Anning's life in a picture-book format.

Bryce, Robert M. *Cook and Peary: The Polar Controversy, Resolved.* Mechanicsburg, PA: Stackpole Books, 1997.

Counter, S. Allen. *North Pole Legacy.* Amherst, MA: The University of Massachusetts Press, 1991.

Dolan, Edward F. Jr. *Matthew Henson, Black Explorer.* New York: Dodd, Mead & Company, 1979.

Earle, Sylvia. *Sea Change: A Message of the Oceans.* New York: G. P. Putnam's Sons, 1995.

Fleming, Fergus. *Barrow's Boys: A Stirring Story of Daring, Fortitude, and Outright Lunacy.* New York: Atlantic Monthly Press, 1998.

John Barrow (1764–1848) dispatched thirty expeditions, some of which were ill-conceived and cost the lives of many heroic British officers unprepared and ill-equipped for their projects. Two of Barrow's obsessions were to find the terminus of the Niger River and, of course, the Northwest Passage. "Barrow's Boys" managed to fill many of the blanks in the map of the world. Roald Amundsen said that reading about the exploits of the Barrow boys inspired him to be an explorer.

Fontaine, Margaret, edited by W. E. Cater. *The Secret Life of a Victorian Lady: Life Among the Butterflies.* Boston, MA: Little, Brown, 1981.

Frank, Katherine. *A Voyage Out: The Life of Mary Kingsley.* Boston, MA: Houghton Mifflin Company, 1986.

Rich in quotes from Kingsley's lively books, letters, and lectures — always informative and often wonderfully humorous — this book helps us understand how brilliant Mary Kingsley, as brave as any male explorer, was so addicted to self-sacrifice and so disdainful of equal rights for women.

Glenn, John. *John Glenn: A Memoir.* New York: Bantam Books, 1999.

Hacker, Carlotta. *Explorers,* Women in Profile Series. New
    York: Crabtree Publishing Company, 1998.

Hall, Mary. *A Woman's Trek from Cape Town to Cairo.*
    London: Methuen, 1907.

Harper, Kenn. *Give Me My Father's Body.* S. Royalton, VT:
    Steerforth Press, 1986.

Haskins, Jim. *Black Eagles: African Americans in Aviation.*
    New York: Scholastic Books, 1995.

Henson, Matthew. *A Black Explorer at the North Pole.*
    Lincoln, NE: First Bison Book, University of Nebraska
    Press, 1989; reprinted from the 1912 edition published
    as *A Negro at the North Pole.*

Huntford, Roland. *The Last Place on Earth.* New York:
    Modern Library, 1999.
The book was first published as *Scott and Amundsen* in England,
1979, with bibliography and careful footnotes, which are not
included in the American edition. The basis of my poem, this
book removes the mythic aura from Scott. It reveals him as in over
his head, especially in comparison to Amundsen. This view was
enforced by the annotated version of *South* by Ernest Shackleton.

Kamler, Kenneth, M.D. *Doctor on Everest.* Foreward by Sir
    Edmund Hillary. New York: The Lyons Press, 2000.

Kennedy, Gregory P. *The First Men in Space.* Foreword by
    Michael Collins. Langhorne, PA: Chelsea House, 1991.

Larner, John. *Marco Polo and the Discovery of the World.*
    New Haven, CT: Yale University Press, 1999.
A fascinating and erudite study of Marco Polo based on versions
and transcriptions of his travels by an expert in medieval
geography. Larner imagines the effect of Marco Polo on his
contemporaries was to give an "extraordinary vision of . . .
unknown cities . . . set within the East."

Maurer, Richard. *The Wild Colorado: The True Adventures of
    Fred Dellenbaugh, Age 17, on the Second Powell
    Expedition into the Grand Canyon.* New York: Crown
    Publishers, Inc., 1999.

Moorehead, Alan. *Darwin and the Beagle.* New York: Harper
    & Row, 1969.
This very readable account of Darwin's five-year voyage as the
naturalist on the *Beagle* is enriched with portraits of Darwin, his
family members, and his colleagues and drawings of the various
exotic people and places seen on the expedition.

Nansen, Fridtjof. *Farthest North.* New York and London:
    Harper & Brothers Publishers, 1898.
Even in translation, Nansen's journal-like telling transports the
reader to the Arctic. He writes with the clarity of a creative
scientist and with a poet's sense of beauty and detail. Even

under difficult times when rations are running low or land isn't where it's supposed to be, Nansen gives a sense of calm thoughtfulness. That same thoughtfulness marks the preparation for the expedition, including the building of Nansen's ship, the *Fram*, which was brilliantly engineered to withstand pack ice as well as provide comfortable living and working space for an arctic voyage of several years. The book gives a sense of the expedition: the hard work, the camaraderie, the frustrations, the tedium, and the distractions, from birthday parties to visiting bears.

Olds, Elizabeth Fogg. *Women of the Four Winds.* Boston, MA: Houghton Mifflin Company, 1985.

Parker, Mary Ann. *A Voyage Round the World in the* Gorgon *Man of War: Captain John Parker.* London: printed by John Nichols, 1795.
This book by a sea captain's wife provides a glimpse of early Australia and South Africa, as well as of naval service. The introductory pages of the book list the subscribers and the book is dedicated by permission to the Princess of Wales.

Parkman, Francis. *La Salle and the Discovery of the Great West.* Boston, MA: Little, Brown and Company, 1903.

Pennington, Piers. *The Great Explorers.* London: Aldus Books Limited: first published in the United States by Facts on File, Inc., 1979.

Polk, Milbry, and Tiegren, Mary. *Women of Discovery.* New York: Clarkson Potter Publishers, 2001.

Reid, Alan. *Discovery and Exploration: A Concise History.* London: Gentry Books, 1980.

Riesenburg, Felix. *Cape Horn.* New York: Dodd Mead & Company, 1939.
Stories of voyagers around Cape Horn, including among others, Magellan, Drake, Fitzroy, Darwin, and Herman Melville. The extensive appendixes have engaging details, such as lore concerning the albatross.

Ride, Sally, with Susan Okie. *To Space & Back.* New York: Lothrop, Lee & Shepard Books, 1986.

Robinson, Jane. *Wayward Women: A Guide to Women Travelers.* Oxford, England: Oxford University Press, 1990.

Ross, Michael Elsohn. *Exploring the Earth with John Wesley Powell.* Minneapolis, MN: Carolrhoda Books, Inc., 2000.
This account is interwoven with accessible geology lessons that lure readers to examine the earth around them as they learn about Powell's life.

Savours, Ann. *The Search for the Northwest Passage.* New
     York: St. Martin's Press, 1999.
A chronological history by a polar expert, this book has fascinating illustrations, such as a photograph of the kind of moccasins Sir John Franklin's starving crew ate to survive.

Shackleton, Sir Ernest. *South,* edited by Peter King. South
     Pomfret, VT: Trafalgar Square Publishing: first published
     in Great Britain, 1919.
Informative editorial notes in the margins make the story of Shackleton's expedition believable in a way that Frank Hurley's gorgeous, archival photographs do not.

Viola, Herman J., and Margolis, Carolyn, editors, with the
     assistance of Jan S. Danis and Sharon D. Galperin.
     *Magnificent Voyagers: The U.S. Exploring Expedition,
     1838–1842.* Washington, D.C.: Smithsonian Books, 1985.

Waldman, Carl, and Wexler, Alan. *Who Was Who in World
     Exploration.* New York: Facts on File, Inc., 1992.

White, Ann Terry. *The American Indian.* Adapted for young
     readers from *The American Heritage Book of Indians*
     by William Brandon. New York: Random House, 1963.
The book presents a panorama of native life in the Americas and the native peoples conquered by the *conquistadores.*

Whittingham, Richard. *The Rand McNally Almanac of Adventure: A Panorama of Danger and Daring.* Skokie, IL: Rand McNally & Company, 1982.

Zweig, Stephan, translated by Eden and Cedar Paul. *The Story of Magellan.* New York: Viking Press, 1939.
A very readable account of Magellan's life with fascinating appendixes containing the "Contract Concerning the Discovery of the Spice Islands . . . by His Majesty." There's also a record of the costs of Magellan's expedition from the oakum used to caulk the ships and the emery to hone the weapons to the cost of all the foodstuffs and trade goods.

Articles

Abercrombie, Thomas J. "Ibn Battuta, Prince of Travelers." *National Geographic* (December 1991): 2–41.

Bushnell, Richard. "Matthew A. Henson, Arctic Explorer." *Mariah* (winter 1976): p. info unavailable.

Chang, Kenneth. "Why Do the Gods Sleep with the Fishes?" *The New York Times* (12/26/2000): F3.

Gill, John Freeman. "Sun, Ice and Explorers' Graves: Navigating the Northwest Passage." *The New York Times* (2/4/2001): TR11.

Kristol, Nicholas D. "1492: The Prequel." *The New York Times Magazine* (6/8/99): 80.

Lane, Anthony. "Breaking the Waves." *The New Yorker* (April 12, 1999): 96–102.

MacMillan, Admiral Donald B. "Matthew Henson." *The Explorer's Journal* Fiftieth Anniversary Issue 33, no.1 (fall 1955): 28–31.

Marriott, Michael. "Two Years Before the Mast (and the Computer)." *The New York Times* (2/9/99): G9.

Miller, Peter. "John Wesley Powell: Vision for the West." *National Geographic* 185, no. 4 (April 1994): 86-114.

Millman, Lawrence. "Looking for Henry Hudson." *Smithsonian* 39, no. 7 (October 1999): 101-110.

Rossabi, Morris. "All the Khan's Horses." *Natural History* (10/94): 48–57.

Sokolov, Raymond. "Before the Conquest." *Natural History* (8/89): 76-79.
Not only did vegetables and spices from the New World enrich the diets of Europeans, but they in turn introduced olive oil and dairy animals that broadened diets of indigenous people. A feast held by Hernando Cortés and Antonio de Mendoza, the first

viceroy of Mexico, is described course by course, including "heifers, roasted whole and stuffed with chickens and . . . quail and pigeons and ham . . . ."

Taylor, Michael, and Torrens, Hugh S. "Fossils by the Sea: Lyme Regis, England." *Natural History* (10/95): 66-71.

Wilson, Samuel M. "White Legends, Lost Tribes." *Natural History* (9/91): 16-20.
Myths attributed to native people told by nonnative conquerors.

"Deep Sea Diver." *National Geographic for Kids* (9/2001): 18-21.

Video

"To the Moon." NOVA: WGBH Boston, 1999.
The story of the U.S. space program is vividly told by the astronauts, the engineers, and the flight directors.

Index of Titles

Index of First Lines